I0618995

Christmas Angel

Merry Exmas Book 2

Alex Silver

ISBN: 978-1-998885-09-1

Synopsis:

ANGEL:

Since the first night Saint brought me back to his place and blew my mind, he's been a bright spot in my life. When we're together, I'm not Owen and Meg's Pop first, and everything else second. For a few glorious hours, all that matters is the pleasure Saint and I share. No strings and no expectations.

With Christmas approaching, I'm on my last frayed nerve. Between extra shifts at work, final exams, and my evil ex stirring up trouble, it's so tempting to lean on Saint more. He means well, but I'm not used to help that doesn't come with hidden snares. Can I trust his love isn't another gilded cage?

1

Saint:

I don't date. Not since my short-lived marriage to my best friend fell apart. That way, no one can pressure me into faking a romantic attraction that I've never experienced. So I should know better than to become involved with someone I represented through a messy divorce. Except my heart apparently didn't receive the memo. Maybe the magic of Christmas is addling my brain, but Angel has me wondering if this time I can be enough for a lasting love.

Christmas Angel is an M/X single-parent, small-town, hurt/comfort, angsty Christmas romance between an aromantic lawyer and a genderqueer single parent of two. This is the second book in the Merry Exmas duology, but both books can stand alone. CW for Angel's abusive ex, misgendering/mild transphobia from the ex, and parental abandonment (Angel's parents and their ex). Make your yuletide gay with Merry Exmas!

Chapter 1

SAINT (SEPTEMBER 10TH, 2021)

ANGEL IS EVERYWHERE I look tonight, and I keep having to tear my eyes off of them. It's one of Pucker's quarterly queer nights and I'm far from the only one trolling the crowd of familiar faces at the bar for a one-night stand. Living in a small town like Elk's Pass, I know most of the people dancing in the dim lighting of the bar.

The rainbow-hued spotlights strobing over the temporary dance floor can't hide that this is still a sport's bar where the town locals gather to drink and watch hockey. Jerseys and other hockey memorabilia still line the walls, interspersed with huge televisions. The screens are set up so that every seat has a view of the game.

Tonight, half the screens are streaming music videos instead of sports highlights, adding to the club vibe. It's not exactly a transformation, but normally I have to drive an hour out to Hamilton to find easy action. So it's a pleasant treat to have options closer to home. I've just learned to be more careful with expectations when hooking up here in Elk's Pass, the perils of small-town life.

Another peril is running into an old friend's tagalong kid sibling all grown up and dressed to impress. Their skinny jeans hug their ass and a form-fitting vest over a bold floral button up emphasizes their masculine figure. As a teenager, Angel used to trail after my friends and me, annoying their brother, Marcus, to no end. Now, they're gorgeous with their sharp features. Their lithe body entices me with their every movement among the knot of people taking advantage of the music to let loose.

Angel and I have been making eyes at each other all evening while I nursed my beer and they bounced and gyrated on the dance floor. No one else here tonight catches my eye, so I dance my way closer to them, trapped in their thrall.

Back when I represented them in their divorce, their hair was freshly shorn close to their scalp in a celebration of their freedom from a controlling ex. It has grown out in the almost two years since they first reached out to me to help end their marriage. They eye fuck me as they give me a coy little wave, inviting me to approach. They are by far the most alluring person in the bar.

I don't fuck my clients. Not even when they bat those pretty long lashes and look up at me through a curtain of silky, dark mahogany hair. I got them full custody and the lion's share of their marital assets. Which should mean they are strictly off limits. But a part of me really wants to make an exception to that rule for Angel.

Angel holds my gaze as I weave my way through the crowd of gyrating bodies. The dim lighting isn't quite enough to give this gathering the illusion of anonymity. I recognize the guy dancing pressed to their back. Angel isn't my only former client among the dancers.

Another downside to moving home to practice law in the tiny town near the US-Ontario border where I grew up is having to be a jack of all trades. It's an upside too, never a dull day. If I'd stayed in Toronto with the cushy corporate law firm where I interned...well I'd be finding loopholes for rich assholes to get richer instead of helping my community.

And for all Angel's guileless innocence, they needed my help when I represented them. Fucking a client is bad. Fucking a former client doesn't have the best optics, but it's not every day that I meet someone who makes me want to bend my own rules.

Which is why the first words out of my mouth when I find myself grinding against my former client are, "I don't date."

It's a truth that has sent most of my exes running once they realize love will never change the fact that I'm aromantic. That truth nearly crushed me when I realized it about myself. Mostly because accepting that I'm not wired for romance meant also accepting that I will never be what the first great love of my life needs.

Angel loops their arms around my neck, pressing our bodies together, and it's easy to push aside thoughts of their contentious divorce. The bold dancer in my arms is light-years from the timid person who sat in my office desperate to leave a miserable situation.

My own divorce—just a year into my ill-fated marriage to my best friend—was amicable, but it broke my heart to let Carl go. It still breaks me sometimes to know that one day I'm going to lose the closeness I've always shared with him when he finds his forever love. When he does, it won't be in a place like this, the music flowing and my blood rushing at being in the middle of a tight knot of writhing bodies.

Carl is still my best friend. We even bought a duplex together when we moved back home. He's my neighbor and a huge part of my life to this day—another fact that drives away potential dates, which is for the best, really. Every person I've let in since Carl has wanted that romance eventually, so it's better not to let anyone close enough for walking away to hurt either party.

It all amps up the physical attraction thrumming through me at every touch from Angel. Their hands drift down to my biceps before they twist in my arms.

Angel grinds their perfect bubble butt back against me more insistently, and for a moment, I'm not sure if they heard me. Do I need to say it again? Angel grabs my hands and places them firmly on their hips, urging me to press us closer together. My breath catches at how good it feels, how naturally we move together.

Carl lives for the romance that will never come easily for me, but this I can do—use my body to bring a partner pleasure. I don't do flowers just because, or surprise anniversary getaways for two with couple's massages or whatever other trite tripe people expect from their lovers. It's not me and I don't want to force myself into pretzels to make someone else happy. No matter how much I love them. I couldn't make Carl happy as his husband. And I won't lead on someone as sweet as Angel.

I should make sure they heard me, but as I open my mouth to repeat myself, Angel smirks up at me over their shoulder. They look cockier than I've seen them since we were teenagers and they had a puppy love crush on me. It's a relief to see a hint of their former fire back in their gray-blue eyes.

"Good, I don't have time to be dated." They wink at me, saucy as fuck and damn, is that ever hot.

"What are you looking for here?" I ask.

It's hard to believe it's already been over a year since I litigated their divorce. Which means two years since they separated from their ex. We've only seen each other in passing since our official attorney-client relationship ended. That's enough time for this to be okay, right?

"Right now? To feel your hands on me while we dance." They grind their ass against me again and I reflexively grip their sides tighter, guiding the movements.

Angel's hips roll into me, and I have to bite back a moan as we move to the music. It would be so much easier to just forget the consequences and take this at face value. Just enjoy the gorgeous person making me feel good. Except I can't forget that Angel is practically family. Carl's sister's husband's baby sibling. So, family at several removes, but still.

"Stop overthinking it, Saint John." Angel growls, turning in my arms and guiding my hands to the lush curves of their ass. Mm. I'm not going to argue with them. They certainly seem to know what they want from me as they nuzzle into the exposed skin at the open V of my shirt.

"Just Saint." I gasp when their fingers tweak my nipple through my button up. Damn, they are winding me up and I'm already aching to get them alone. "Fuck, you want to drive me wild, Ange?"

Angel flinches, then shakes their head. They try to soften the reaction, wrinkling their nose at me—looking adorable as fuck—as they firmly correct the nickname. "Angel."

"Got it. Angel," I repeat. They're still plastered against my body. I'm so hard. All I really want is to take them home and fuck them as senseless as they're making me. I'm ready to throw caution to the winds. "Would you want to get out of here and get horizontal?"

"I'd ask your place or mine, but it has to be your place because my kids are at mine."

"Alone?" Stupid question, and none of my business. Their eldest must be practically teenaged by now. Damn, time flies.

Angel shakes their head.

"I hired a sitter. So you better make this worth her hourly rate." Angel winks at me.

I laugh at their audacity. "I'll do my best. You know I'm not going to fall in love with you and make all your problems go away, right?"

Angel snorts, like I'm talking out my ass and presses a finger to my lips. They plaster their body to mine, their chest is all angular planes leaving no space between us as I hold them in my arms. The transition they put off for years for the sake of a broken marriage looks good on them. They seem happier like this, cheekbones more prominent, the barest hint of a downy mustache over their kissable lips, so much quicker to smile than I remember.

They're sure of themself as we dance. Irresistibly confident. It's like they've carved away all the parts that used to make them hide at the edges of our group with hunched shoulders. Reticent, even before their ex hooked his claws into them.

"The only problem I need you to solve is that I don't remember the last time I had a really good fuck."

I nibble at the finger still pressed to my lips. When Angel makes no move to pull away, I suck the tip into my mouth, giving them the barest

8

hint of what's in store back at my place. Angel's eyes flutter shut and they moan before pulling their hand free.

"Well, that is a problem I am more than happy to fix for you." I wink.

Angel laughs, stepping out of my arms. They trail their fingers down my arm to take my hand. With our eyes still locked, they maneuver us to the edge of the dance floor so we can settle our tabs and leave.

The entire drive home, I keep glancing in my rearview to be sure their ancient old beater of a car is still behind me. Angel parks on the street in front of my duplex. They grin when I fumble with my keys because I'm too busy staring at their approach to pay attention to what I'm doing. Once we're finally inside, they quirk a brow at me. "Nice digs. Show me the bedroom?"

I shut the door between us and the rest of the world, and it's like we can't keep our mouths and hands to ourselves. I strip off their silky shirt and kiss their sharp collarbones. They tug my shirt off too, heedless of the fiddly buttons, so it's just as well I had enough of them unfastened to make that easy. We keep kissing and touching all the way up the stairs, shedding clothing as we go, until we're naked in my room and Angel pulls me down onto the mattress.

"Want you on top of me, condom if you want to fuck me. I've got an IUD, but I'm *not* risking another kid or anything else."

"Got it." I chuckle as I reach over to grab a condom from the side table. "Not looking for anyone to call me Daddy. Unless that floats your boat?"

Angel licks their lips, eyes darting over me. "Not tonight."

"Sure." I rake my gaze over their tantalizing body. "Do we need something for oral? I could probably cut open a condom to use as a dental dam."

Angel shrugs, their hair bunching around their shoulders with the motion. "I'm okay risking unprotected oral if you are, I haven't been with anyone since my last test."

That's good enough for me, sure there's still a risk, but I want to taste them. "Anything else I should know about what you like?"

"Not the biggest fan of anal." They don't meet my eyes as they say it and they seem tense even talking about it. I don't miss how they're reticent to give a firm no, so anal's definitely off the table tonight. "You can fuck my front bits."

That last part they seem more into. I stroke my thumb along the shaft of their clit, enjoying the way they arch into the touch and how the foreskin moves over the swollen head. Hmm, actually, I should probably ask what terms they prefer.

"What do I call this?" I rub them again for emphasis.

"I call it Bitsy. No anatomical terms, please." Angel bites their lip. "Mm, keep doing that."

"Does Bitsy like it?" I tease, wondering if they're cool with me fingering them to get my fingers nice and wet—only one way to find out. "Can I finger you, darling?"

"Mhm."

I kiss them as I trace their opening with two fingers. They seem into it, but we're probably going to need lube for this. Between the size of Bitsy and the dryness between their folds, I'm pretty sure they're on testosterone. But it's not really any of my business unless they want to talk about their transition.

"You good to come more than once, Angel?"

"Yeah." They gasp and nod. "Don't stop."

"I've got you. Just relax and let me take care of you, yeah?" I've got plenty of lube, and all night to make this good. I take my time working my way down their body. As I stretch Angel open with lube, I suck on Bitsy. It's not long before every thrust of my fingers makes filthy, squelching sounds. They're already bucking into my mouth with broken little moans and pleas for more.

This is one of my favorite parts of sex. The raw vulnerability of pleasure. How Angel grips my silky soft sheets in their fists, the arch of their back as they strain against my face. The soft sounds they can't hold back. The way they gasp my name as they come for the first time with my mouth around Bitsy and my fingers buried inside them.

Next time I'm going to watch their face when they come undone. I want to see their eyes flutter shut, or go all soft and unfocused. I want to memorize their pleasure. For now, it's enough to feel every wave of their release clenching around my fingers. Mm. That's going to feel incredible around my cock when I make them come again.

I don't pull away until Angel relaxes under me with a last full body shiver.

"Good?" I wipe the back of my hand over my mouth and crawl back up their body.

"Uh huh." Angel's smile is radiant, but it dims a bit when they glance down at us and see that I'm still hard. They drape their forearm over their eyes to hide their expression. "Give me a second?"

"Take all the time you want, Angel. I can take care of myself if you aren't up for another round."

"No, just. Sorry."

"No sorries needed. You can say no to anything with me, darling." I can't help stroking their cheek. They peek up at me through their splayed fingers, reading my face like their safety depends on it. If I didn't already hate their ex, that right there would clinch it. I can see the sorry on the tip of their tongue, so I press my finger to their lips. "Nope. No sorries."

"I wasn't gonna." They bark out a laugh and nip at my fingertip. It's a lie, but that's okay. I'm just happy to see them confident enough to be playful with me. I flop onto my back beside Angel so I'm not hovering over them, like I expect something. This first taste was enough for now. Enough to make me sure I want more than one night with them to learn all their quirks and the things that turn them on.

Angel rolls onto their side, propping their chin on their palm. They gaze at me as they trace idle fingers over my chest, twirling them in my chest hair. They tug and the little pinpricks of pain make me hiss out a breath. It's easy for them to take my breath away; they're so damn sexy.

"Sorry." Angel cringes. "Sor—I didn't—"

I capture their lips in a kiss to forestall them. "It's fine. We'll practice not apologizing for every little thing."

"It might take a lot of practice," they admit wryly.

"Hm, guess we'll have to do this again." I smile at them.

"Yeah?" Angel sounds painfully hopeful.

"Yeah." I pet their silky hair.

"Shit." Angel cringes at the sight of something past my shoulder. "Even if I said I have to leave?"

I follow their gaze to the time on my alarm clock.

"Do you have to get home?" I do my best to hide my disappointment.

"Don't hate me?" Angel bites their lip, eyes still on my clock, and nods. "Mira charges double if I'm out past midnight. And I have to get the kids to school in the morning. Sor—"

"Nope, no sorry." I press my finger to their lips to cut off their apology. "Tempting as a hate fuck might be, you're going to have to do much worse than being a responsible parent to make me hate you. Give me one more kiss and go home to your kids. I won't hold anything against you, okay?"

"Well, I want you to hold your body against me." They try to match my levity as they roll out of bed and start the search for their clothes. I get up too, pulling on comfy flannel pajama bottoms to get my erection out of their sight so they'll stop worrying about it.

"Next time," I promise. Hopefully, there will be a next time. One little taste of Angel isn't nearly enough.

"Really? Even though you didn't get anything out of this?" They gesture at my crotch as they pull on their silky underwear.

"I got to make my gorgeous friend come."

"Yeah, but..."

"You missed how hard that made me?" I quirk a brow at them.

Angel shakes their head and laughs nervously. "That's my point..."

"Darling, if I cared that much about sticking my dick in you, then I'd have started with that."

"I didn't realize how late it was." They sneak in another apology as I trail them down the hall to their discarded pants. I let that one pass in favor of watching them. They're hot as they jiggle their ass into the skintight denim. They glance back over their shoulder at me, and I don't think they have a clue how alluring they are.

I shake my head, smiling at them. "When can I see you again?"

They pause, consider me. "You really want to do this again?"

"I really want to make you come again." I wink at them. These things are always a delicate balance between making my ongoing interest clear without leading anyone on about my intentions.

"Thursdays. Both kids have evening activities. So I usually have a few hours free."

They look around for their shirt and spot it at the bottom of the stairs. I keep following them, gathering up my laundry along the way.

"Okay. You still have my number?"

"Yeah. Somewhere."

"Call me if anything changes, otherwise I'll expect you Thursday around five?"

"Six." The correction is muffled through the fabric of their shirt as they put it back on and hastily fasten the tiny buttons.

"Even better, I'll expect you at sex o'clock," I tease.

They giggle at the corny as fuck joke. "See you then, Saint." They pause in front of the door, gaze locked onto my lips.

I walk up to them, brace a hand against the wall, making sure to leave them an escape route if they aren't into being caged in, and kiss them goodbye. I brush a finger over their glossy lips. "Good night, Angel."

Then I step back, pulling the door open and gesturing for them to go.

They give me one more longing glance over their shoulder before jogging to their car and leaving me to jerk off to the memory of them in my bed.

Chapter 2

ANGEL (SEPTEMBER 15TH 2023)

"HEY, ANGEL." SAINT GREETS me at the door with his most charming grin. I didn't bother to pack an overnight bag, even though I have every intention of waking up in his bed tomorrow. There's a toothbrush by his sink with my name on it for the rare occasions when I can stay over. It's nice to sleep together after we fuck and Saint is a cuddler.

I wasn't up for making a stop at home after work, and the kids would have asked questions if I threw my overnight bag into the trunk along with theirs. Trevor picked them up from the diner because I had a dinner shift and he was running late, as usual. But I'm not here to dwell on that mess. I'm here to get railed.

I drag Saint into a kiss. It's sloppy since I'm toeing off my shoes as his lips part for my tongue.

"Mmph." Saint stops trying to talk. His hands settle on my hips, then slide around to cup my ass, drawing me against his body. The familiar press of his firm chest against mine has me groaning. I rock into his erection. He swallows my moans. Saint's tongue moving over mine makes me hyper aware of all the other places he's so very good at kissing.

Most of the time, I only get to see Saint on Thursdays. It's the one day of the week when both of my kids' after-school activities align and I can take two glorious hours to be selfish. I've guarded that time like a dragon hoarding jewels for the better part of two years now. It's harder in the summer, when the kids are out of school, but I've been making it work. Meg offered to babysit her little brother a few times over the past couple of months for extra spending money. And I'm not above arranging sleepovers with their friends to get a little me time. Still, it's been nice having them back on their usual schedules with school back in session.

And as of suppertime, they are officially with their father for the next two nights. Which is why I have no intentions of leaving Saint's bed until I have to get ready for my next shift at work.

Saint pins me against the wall and works his hand into the front of my pants. Two fingers stroke me until Bitsy is achingly hard and I'm desperate to have him inside me. Not quite desperate enough for a wall fuck, because that shit sounds hotter than it is when you have to balance staying upright with getting plowed, but almost. It's fine though, we can get a much better angle in bed. We kiss and grope our way across Saint's living room, up the stairs, and down the hall into his room.

I toss my clothes into a heap on the floor once we're in his room. It's amazing to shed the scents of the diner's kitchen, greasy food and industrial cleaner, that always seem to cling to me after work. I'm so glad to be rid of them.

Saint watches me like he hasn't seen every inch of me naked. Like I'm something to behold, stretch marks, scars, and all. I'm not, but he sure is. My mouth waters at his toned abs as he strips out of his shirt. I want to lick my way up his body to his sculpted pecs and strong shoulders. Instead, I plop down on the edge of his mattress to watch him step out of his pants and boxers. His dick is a work of art, bobbing in front of him with every step he takes toward me.

He steps between my thighs, and I spread for him. His hands rest on my shoulders as I tilt my face up to his. He trails his fingers along my throat as we kiss. I shiver when his cock rubs against Bitsy. Saint moans and pushes me onto my back. He follows me down to the bed, still kissing as we rut our groins together.

"Mm, oh, right there?" I buck up into him, grinding the sensitive head of my bits against the flared ridge of his cock head.

Saint obliges me, meeting my desperate humping with a smile. "You're so sexy when you get yourself off."

His praise makes me falter, but Saint shifts to grab my hip in one hand and urges me to keep going. "Come on. Ride my cock, darling. Make yourself feel good."

I can't help giving in to the command in his voice. He makes it easy to surrender myself to the pursuit of pleasure. Each thrust sends heat spangling through my core. I'm so close and it's so good, but I don't really want him jizzing all over my bits.

He rolls his hips, dragging his hard cock in a smooth glide over Bitsy's length. Ugh. I don't want him to stop, but we should definitely get him suited up with his dick already dribbling precum over me. My bits are all tingly and wet for him. Or as wet as they get these days, with testosterone drying things out down below. It is well worth needing a little extra lube, for the way Bitsy has grown since I started the low dose injections.

"Condom." I gasp. Saint is always diligent about using them when he fucks me. I just need him in me right fucking now.

"So impatient. We've got all night for once, darling. You that eager for this to be over?" Saint teases me as he lifts onto his elbows to reach for the bedside table where he keeps his supplies.

"No. But—" I kiss him, lightly scraping my teeth over his lower lip. "—mhm, want you." I groan when he pulls away enough to actually grab the foil packet. I pout as he kneels up to roll on the latex.

"You've got me." Saint flashes his brilliant grin again. "Just a second."

"Ugh, you are such a tease." I stroke myself as I watch him spread more lube onto his cock. I want his dexterous fingers on me. Saint watches me with that playful, knowing smirk of his. He can be such a tease. So I'm not surprised when he continues to take his time. Saint draws out the display with exaggerated porno faces and moaning over his own hand. When I've humored his theatrics long enough, I crunch upright to wrap my fingers around his nape and haul him laughing down to cover me.

"Oh, did you want something?" Saint wriggles, so the smooth tip of his cock paints lube all over my crotch. The brush of his light touch is tantalizingly inadequate. I wrap my legs around him, pinning him closer. Saint laughs against my lips. I grind into him, turning his laughter into a moan as the head of his dick presses against my entry. I shift, opening to him and pushing against him until he slips inside.

"Mm, you feel incredible, darling." He mouths along my jaw to whisper into my ear. I shudder as he moves inside of me. Everything is slick and warm and so good. I keep touching myself while he thrusts into me, his ragged breathing mingles with mine and I capture his lips, enjoying the sensuality of being fucked slow and gentle. Like we have all the time in the world, because for once we do.

Sex with Saint is always amazing. But when our eyes meet and our bodies are moving in this slow synchrony, it's unbearably sweet. Like he can tear me open and see straight to my most vulnerable core and I can't handle it. His pace falters, and I'm pretty sure he's just as haunted by the specter of might-have-beens neither of us can face. We aren't a couple, and this gentle intimacy is too close to what that might look like if we didn't both have our reasons for keeping sex and emotions separate.

"Fuck me like you mean it, Saint." I rake my blunt nails over his shoulders, arching into him. I need to break the tension. Saint seems relieved by the shift in mood from that cloyingly sweet, quiet intensity.

"I thought you'd never ask, Angel." Saint winks at me. Then he bends me in half and fucks me like it's a race to get off. Fucking me like this. It's probably going to be him. Either way, we've been doing this for long enough that I know he'll make sure I'm satisfied before we're done. "Want me to come inside you or pull out, darling? Come all over that handsome face?"

"Ungh, no jizz in my hair." I grimace up at him, grunting with the effort of meeting his thrusts.

He's wearing a condom and I've still got my IUD in place. So he can come wherever he wants as long as he doesn't stop what his hand is doing to Bitsy and I don't have to clean up after him.

Saint laughs, hard enough that his rhythm falters and he pulls out of me, burying his face in my shoulder as he jerks himself to stay hard. "Gotcha. Don't make a mess."

"Mhm, I'm officially off the clock for cleaning up other people's bodily fluids." I sigh as the coiled pleasure low in my belly eases, my orgasm drifting further out of reach as Saint chuckles until his eyes are watering.

"It wasn't *that* funny." I pout, put out at having my pleasure evaporate so close to climax. Edging bastard.

"It was though. You should have seen your face." Saint wipes tears from the crinkles he gets around his eyes when he really smiles. He's so freaking joyful it's unreal sometimes. "Damn, you are such a parent."

I swat playfully at his shoulder, torn between amusement and frustration. "Is that supposed to be pillow talk? You normally don't suck at it this much."

"Come here and I'll show you how much I suck." Saint beckons teasingly. I squirm toward him.

Saint manhandles me so that he's between my splayed open thighs again, this time leaning over me to take Bitsy into his mouth. He lathes me with his tongue. My irritation floats away on waves of bliss.

I reach for Saint, and he shifts position so that I can wrap a fist around his hard dick while he blows my mind. I come first after all, but only just. Saint thrusts hard into my fist as he comes right after me, lips still sealed around my shaft. His low moaning as he climaxes vibrates through me, his tongue coaxing a few more shuddering jerks of pleasure out of me.

Once we catch our breath, Saint gets up to deal with the used condom and returns to his bed with a warm washcloth to tidy our mess. We snuggle naked in his bed. His fingers play idly over my body as we catch up on the mundane details of each other's lives. It's the abridged version, like I'd share over drinks if I had the sort of adult friends I grew up watching on television. Mostly, we try to make each other smile.

He pinches my nipple as he tells me about a client who won't stop emailing him off the wall estate planning questions at all hours. I wriggle my ass against Saint's limp cock as I tell him about the last few classes I need to pass before I can begin my student teaching in the spring. He chuckles at the corny math jokes my one professor posts at the start of each lecture. In his arms, I can't stop smiling. I don't have to worry about the hard things—other than his dick still nestled cozy against my ass—and that's almost as good as the sexual release.

As we chat, we idly explore each other's bodies. Familiar as that territory has become over our stolen nights together, it feels incredible to touch and be touched. His hands have me getting turned on all over again by the time his dick is nudging insistently against me. I hook my leg over his hip, handing him another condom for round two. Fucking me from behind—with both of us dozy—his gentle thrusts don't feel quite as intimate as they did earlier, face-to-face.

Saint rocks into me, and we take our time savoring the sweet pleasure until we both come. I shift around enough to let him handle the aftermath. We fall asleep with him still draped around me. Visions of waking up to leisurely morning sex and sharing my morning coffee with an actual adult flicker behind my closed eyelids. Hard to say which I'm looking forward to more.

MY RINGTONE JOLTS ME awake in the wee hours of the night, dashing my hopes of a lazy morning. Disoriented, I roll out of Saint's bed to get my phone. Shit. It's my ex. If it wasn't his weekend with our kids, I'd reject his call out of hand. But if something is wrong with Owen or Meg... I can't risk missing an emergency with my kids. A text pops up before I can swipe to answer the phone call.

Meg: Come get us plz? Owen's rly sick. *puke emoji*

My stomach drops. I want to ask her if he's okay, but I need to answer the call and I can ask her father rather than put her in the middle.

Pops: OMW

I tap out a quick reply to assure my daughter that I'm on my way first, then take the call before it goes to voicemail.

"Is everything alright?" I hiss into the phone, glancing at Saint to be sure I haven't woken him.

He looks lovely in the moonlight, his chiseled jaw just begs to be kissed. I'm not sure how I've kept his interest for over a year now.

He's so kind and so out of my league. Sculpted muscles that I've had my hands all over since we started hooking up. I love his salt and pepper hair that makes him look distinguished and older than his not quite forty years. The laugh lines around his eyes that mark his good nature faded in sleep, but still visible.

I like that he smiles so much. It gives me hope that I can smile that much too. For the handful of hours I steal with him each week, I get to.

"Owen puked," Trevor says.

I don't flinch at the disgust in his voice. The lack of empathy is nothing new. He's not calling because he's concerned that our son is sick; he's calling because he doesn't want to deal with the inconvenience. This won't be a quick call I can handle and slip back into bed with my sometimes lover.

"Did you get him cleaned up?" I ask.

22

I give Saint one last wistful glance. Then I slip back into last night's clothes to leave as Trevor unloads at me, calling me every name in the book for even asking. He complains about how gross puke is and how it's somehow my fault Owen is sick. At least if he's complaining to me, he isn't directing his ire at Owen. So much for having one night to myself.

"What do you want me to do about it?" I finally break into Trevor's tirade to ask.

I already know. It's only going to give him more ammunition to throw at me when I show up in last night's clothing fresh from the floor to pick up the kids.

"Fuck, he's puking again! Come get the brats. It's only a matter of time before Meg starts up too, with Owen this sick. You're draining me dry with child support as it is. I can't afford to miss work if they infect me. Besides, there's no point having them here if they're just going to be puking."

I pinch the bridge of my nose to hold back the retort that the point is for him to step up and be a fucking parent to his kids. That wouldn't be productive. The burning ember of resentment in the center of my chest cools to weary resignation. Trevor has no desire to change. Hence the divorce. I just wish he could step up for the kids, even though he couldn't be a decent partner for me.

"Sure. I'm on my way."

It's too much to ask that he have them ready when I get there. At least I only have to deal with him for his custody weekends twice a month. And half the time he doesn't even show up for those.

I'm probably an asshole for being glad of that when it makes Owen sad and Meg bitter, but better an absent dad than one who blames them for getting sick. Fuck. I wish...well, a lot of things. Mostly, I wish I was already holding my sick kiddo, cozy at home.

When I show up, Trevor answers the door in his boxers.

"Your mom's here." He curls his lip in a sneer at the skimpy black dress I'm wearing.

I didn't bother with the torn nylons, so my hairy legs are on full display. He doesn't have to say a word for me to know all the things he'd say if Meg, our fourteen-year-old, wasn't standing there with her and Owen's overnight bags.

"Hey, Meg." I wave to my kid, ignoring the misgendering. I'm used to that level of petty from my ex, so I keep my mouth shut rather than stoking the flames. Away from him, it's easier to embrace the side of me that is becoming secure enough in my masculinity to still enjoy dressing in pretty things like the comfy dress I wore to work last night.

"Hey, Pop," Meg says, her own small defiance to the way Trevor treats me.

Her eyes light up when she sees me and I wish I could just hug her, but she jumps up and whirls to head down the hall. I hate that she ends up in the middle of our shit like this.

"I'll go get Owen," Meg calls over her shoulder.

"How is he?" I ask, standing on the porch since Trevor hasn't made any move to let me in.

Trevor rolls his eyes. "He puked twice more since I called. I'm going to be up all night doing laundry."

"Does he have a fever?"

"How should I know?"

Right. I'll have to check when we get home. I bite my tongue. Nothing good will come of pushing for details. "Want them to call you to set up a raincheck?"

"No. And I'll be out of town for my next visit, so I'll take them again for the October long weekend. Mom is planning to drive down from Hamilton to stay in town with us."

"Sure." I grit my teeth at his cavalier treatment of our custody arrangement. "I'll text you to confirm."

It will be good for the kids to see their grandma, even if it's not supposed to be his weekend. I don't have a problem with Trevor's mom. Sure, we had our rocky times, but I know she adores Meg and Owen and dotes on them.

My ex-mother-in-law took me in when I was eighteen and pregnant with her granddaughter after my folks kicked me out because they didn't approve of my relationship with Trevor. Ironic that their cutting me off is the main reason I ended up married to the asshole.

Owen and Meg come back down the hall, and my little boy looks miserable. His cheeks have a grayish pallor and his eyes a febrile glow. When he sees me, he throws himself at me and I drop to my haunches to scoop him into my arms. I smother him in kisses and brush sweat-lank hair from his fevered brow.

"Pop, I don't feel good."

"I know, baby." I lift him into my arms. He's getting too big for this. Owen's lanky legs dangle past my knees when I hold him now, but I'm going to cling on as long as I can. I glance at Trevor and try to ignore his scowl at my 'coddling' our son. He's only nine, at least for a few more weeks. Of course I'm going to coddle him when he's sick. Fuck Trevor for not doing the same. I bite back my anger and just say, "Text me when you're ready to arrange October."

"Sure. Bye, kids." Trevor spits out the words like a censure for them not saying it first.

"Bye, Daddy," Owen mumbles into my neck, clinging to me like he used to when he was my sweet little toddler.

"Bye," Meg says sullenly, hefting both kids' bags and following me out the door.

I carry Owen to the car—he's going to be too big for me to carry him at all soon—and buckle him into his booster seat. Meg tosses the bags in on the other side, then buckles into the front passenger seat. She's already got her nose buried in her phone, probably texting friends that she'll be home ahead of schedule.

I rummage for a bag or something in case Owen gets sick again, but I just cleaned everything out of the car. The best I can do is to throw the old blanket I keep in here for emergencies over his lap to contain any potential messes.

"Aim for this if you feel sick on the way home, alright?" I tuck the thin fleece over him and brush my fingers over his feverish brow. My poor little guy just gives me a feeble nod.

I get behind the wheel and try not to worry about just how sick Owen might be.

"How was it?" I ask as I pull out of Trevor's driveway.

"Eh? Dad was Dad. Do we have to go to his place?" Meg's shoulders hunch, and I wish I had a different answer to give her.

"I can't deny him access to you kids." I give her a tight smile and resolve to ask Saint if Meg can refuse to go. Or if that will be just as bad as when I wanted to renege on Trevor's court-ordered visitation.

"It's not like he actually wants to see us."

Owen moans in the back. "I'm gonna—"

"Aim for the blanket, if you can." I squeeze the steering wheel as he hurls all over the back seat. Fuck. At least his timing saves me from saying something ill-advised about their father. When I glance in the rearview, it looks like he mostly hit the blanket.

"It's okay, baby, let it out. We'll be home in a minute and we can get you cleaned up and into bed," I soothe.

"Gross." Meg rolls down her window at the stench of vomit.

Owen starts crying.

"You're okay, baby. Just hold on a few more minutes." I keep driving, going as fast as I dare on quiet residential streets in the middle of the night. Cleaning the barf blanket properly will have to wait until tomorrow.

I'm going to have to call in sick for the extra weekend shifts I took since I wasn't supposed to have the kids. I promised Meg she wouldn't be my built-in-babysitter and I'm not asking her to care for her brother when he's this sick. Damn it all. So much for a bit of breathing room on the bills. That's a problem for later.

I focus on taking care of Owen, giving him store brand Tylenol and Gravol and getting him tucked into bed in clean PJs. I make sure he has a bucket in case he gets sick again and a bottle of generic sports drink to keep him hydrated.

Meg goes to her room, purportedly to sleep, but there's every chance she's venting to her friends about the short-lived visit with her father. I need to check in with her properly, but there's only one of me and I have to focus on the kid who needs me more right now. Some days it seems like all I do is triage disasters.

I hold Owen as he shivers and he clings to me like he used to. Even though he's sick, I savor this vestige of his childhood. I know from Meg that I've only got so much longer when my baby is going to want to snuggle.

Eventually, his fever breaks, and he falls into an exhausted slumber. It's been a few hours since he last vomited. I collapse into my own bed as dawn is breaking over the horizon. And if I wish I had someone to hold me and whisper soothing words—someone like Saint, with laugh lines and so much authority in every syllable that I can't help but believe him when he tells me everything will be okay—well, that might as well be a fever dream.

Chapter 3

SAINT (SEPTEMBER 21ST, 2023)

IT'S QUARTER PAST SIX on a Thursday, and I'm getting antsy waiting for the knock on my front door. We've been doing this for over two years now. Angel being late is nothing new. There's a pesky voice at the back of my head that's flashing warning lights about how invested I am in this. It never ends well when I get too used to a usual hookup.

Expectations and feelings always enter in at some point and I'm just not built for flowers and forevers. Which means I do my best not to show too much affection that might send mixed signals about what I want. But Angel has so much else on their plate, they seem safe to let myself fall into routines with. Safe to care about.

Sometimes I just want a steady partner. Someone like Carl, who isn't going to push me for more than I can give, only with sex. Angel is the closest I've come to finding that since they're juggling school, work, and being a single parent.

Thursdays are our one consistent time together since both kids have overlapping activities now that school is back in session and they have a more regular schedule. Meg has dance and usually hangs out with her friends after her class, and Owen goes to tae kwon do. Between training and sparring with his competition team, he'll be busy for at least two hours. Which means for the next two hours, Angel is all mine.

Except they're later than usual, darn it. I've been looking forward to our time together all week. After they ran out on our sleepover last Friday, I'm a weird combination of horny and worried about how they're doing.

Their loud rap on my door startles me. I lunge for the door, tearing it open, then try to salvage any iota of suaveness by leaning on it as I drink them in. None the worse for wear. Or at least, no worse than usual. Their eyes look as tired as ever and their long hair is unwashed and pulled back into a messy man bun that screams of not enough hours in a day.

They pounce on me, arms around my neck, pulling my face down for a kiss. I smile against their lips, reassured by their eagerness.

"Fuck, I need this tonight, you have no idea," Angel mumbles as they crowd me up against the hall closet. I barely get the door closed before they're fishing my dick out of my pants.

"Shit, your hands are cold," I protest, nudging their hand away from my junk. Angel slumps and I hate myself for the dejected way they won't quite look at me.

"Sorry," they mumble, hugging themself.

I pull them into an embrace. "It's fine, Angel. Let's get you warmed up first, shall we?" I rub between their legs, making my offer as clear as day. They bite their lip before nodding. I'd like to bite there too. Their makeup emphasizes their more masculine jawline lately. When they haven't shaved in a few days, I like the feel of their downy soft facial hair. It's several shades lighter than the dark hair on their head so that it's not super obvious. They aren't a fan of that little color quirk, but it's kind of adorable. Like everything else about them.

"Bed?" Angel asks.

"Yeah." I sweep my arm toward the stairs and my bedroom.

Angel leads the way. They drop onto my bed, legs splayed wide and watch me with wide, trusting eyes. "How do you want me?"

"All the ways, darling. But let's start with naked."

Angel rolls their eyes as they stand to wriggle out of their leggings. Mm, there's nothing but skin underneath the thin fabric. Their long, flowy shirt brushes their thighs and gives me enticing glimpses of Bitsy with their every movement.

I nudge them back down onto the mattress and kneel between their legs. The position gives me access to kiss all over their inner thighs. I don't stop teasing them until they beg me to suck them, fingers tangled in my hair.

I take my time slurping them into my mouth. Angel moans, rocking against me. I pin them in place and draw out their pleasure with languid strokes and swirls of my tongue. It takes me a while to realize that the sweet moans have trailed off into snores.

I laugh at the absurdity of them falling asleep with my face buried between their thighs. They mumble a sleepy protest when I get up and tuck them into my bed before setting an alarm and curling up next to them.

They clearly need the sleep, and I've been craving their skin against mine. This is almost as good as sex. Sleeping together is one of those little boundaries I rarely cross with hookups. It muddles things, and when I need the comfort of a nice cuddle session, I've got Carl..

Sex is easy. Opening up to an emotional connection when I know I can't be what most people expect from a relationship is more complicated. But Angel hasn't pushed for 'more' and I already cared about them before we started whatever this situationship is between us.

I can hold someone I care about without it meaning anything deeper than that we both needed the contact with another human being. It seems like I've barely shut my eyes when the alarm wakes Angel with a start.

"Fuck. I fell asleep?" They blink blearily at me.

I wish I could tuck them into my bed and let them rest for as long as they need. Until the permanent bags under their eyes are gone, at least. But someone has to pick up their kids and it can't be me. I'm not their boyfriend to step into that partner role and I sure as shit don't want their kids to get attached when I inevitably have to end this. Bad enough to risk Angel's heart for my selfishness in holding onto them. I'm not dragging their kids into this. If they'd even allow that.

They shove my shoulder, clearly peeved with me. "Damn it, why didn't you wake me up?"

"You clearly needed sleep more than a fuck." I shrug, not the least bit apologetic. It's not like I was going to shake them awake to insist on getting my dick wet. And they know me better than to think I would by now.

Angel sits up, pressing the heels of their hands to their eyes, and erupts into bitter laughter that sounds on the verge of sobbing. Their shoulders heave and maybe I do feel a little bad that they're upset, even if I stand by letting them get what rest they could. "Yeah. Well, now I'm not going to get either of those things."

I pat their back, consoling them awkwardly. "I'm sorry?"

Angel groans and uncovers their face to scowl at me. Damn, I enjoy seeing them fired up and standing their ground, even if it is because I've frustrated them. "I thought there was a rule against apologies in this bed?" They sulk, pouting at me.

"That only applies to you." I boop their nose and capture their lips in a gentle kiss on the lips that I've missed getting the chance to kiss properly again until next week.

It's on the tip of my tongue to offer them help. Whatever they need—as a friend. Except I know most friends don't offer that sort of blank cheque support to their fuck buddies with no strings or conditions. Getting involved connotes relationship things I'm not prepared to offer anyone, not even Angel. I'm already blurring so many of the lines with them. I can't.

It kills me to even float my next tentative offer, but if I'm taking up time they need for other things, it might be the best I can give them. "Do we need to take a break?" I rake my fingers through my hair, holding my breath with the hope they'll refuse.

"No!" Angel's eyes widen, hurt quickly hidden behind their intensifying scowl. "Please don't take this away from me, Mathieu Saint John. I'm fine. It's just rough getting back into the school routine and picking up some extra shifts."

I can read between the lines of what they just said well enough. They have to pay for their classes, coursework that they could have finished ages ago if they could attend school full time instead of tackling their degree in dribs and drabs spread over years. The kids must have needed supplies and probably new clothes. And this is the time of year when their activity fees renew, if I'm correctly recalling the financial statements I have no business remembering years after handling their divorce.

"Is he paying the child support on time?" I ask, clenching my hands into fists to stop myself from reaching for them. Angel looks like any scrap of comfort might break open the floodgates right now. I'm not prepared to hold myself at the essential emotional distance to avoid entanglements if I let them sob on my shoulder tonight. Much as part of me wants to be the friend they can cry to.

"Ha!" Angel scoffs at my question. "He hasn't paid in a while, Saint. Quit his job at the bank and started working construction for cash under the table ages ago."

Well, that at least I can help with. "That's something you tell your lawyer about, Angel."

"What lawyer? I can't afford to pay you, Saint. And I don't want to."

"Why not?" I demand, unable to disguise my offense at the slight to my professional pride. "I thought you were happy with the terms I got you?"

Angel gives me a look like I'm missing something obvious and then gestures between us, naked in my bed. "Um, because I'm pretty sure you aren't the sort of professional who sleeps with his clients? I know you don't do relationships, but fuck buddies are still probably a conflict of interest? Or at least morally ambiguous."

Oh. Right. That's a solid point. Maybe I'm more than a bit addled when it comes to Angel. "I can still send a threatening letter on your behalf to get him to pay up." I pout.

Angel kisses my cheek, then pats it.

"Don't bother, can't get blood from a stone. I did have a lawyerly question for you though. If that's okay?"

They pick at the blankets.

"Go ahead."

"Meg says she doesn't want to go with Trevor on his weekends. Can she refuse, or will that cause problems?"

I shake my head, wishing I could give them the answer they want to hear. "It's not up to her, unfortunately. She can tell him no if he's alright with missing the time, or rescheduling, but if he wants to push the issue, he could make an alienation case against you."

"Even though he's way behind on his child support, skips most of his time anyway, and Meg is fourteen now?" Angel presses, though I suspect they already know the answer.

"Yeah. I wish I could tell you she gets to make her own decisions about where she spends her time, but as long as she's a minor, it's complicated. Unless her safety is a concern?"

Angel hesitates. "No. He wouldn't actually hurt them."

I raise my eyebrow. "Elaborate?"

Angel rolls their eyes. "He talks a lot of shit, but he wouldn't physically harm the kids. Neglect at worst? And Meg has her phone to call me if she or Owen need anything while they're with him."

"Okay. Document when he misses his visits, so you have proof that you are making every effort to encourage a relationship with the kids. Just in case."

"Yeah. I document everything with him. Even if he tells me verbally, I text him what we discussed afterward. Drives him nuts, but I learned my lesson from the trial." Angel purses their lips.

"Good." I kiss them. "You're doing everything you can."

"Thanks." Angel sighs. "Damn, I feel like I should pay you for that."

I snort. "Yeah, I bill all my friends for shit I could tell them in my sleep."

They stick out their tongue at me. "Uh huh, and you sleep with all your friends, too, so they can just overhear all that sound legal advice you apparently dream about?"

"Obviously. Why do you think I have so many good friends?" I try to sound flippant about it, but it's my turn to look away, because yeah, I kind of do sleep with most of my friends. In the sense that Carl is my closest friend and we still sometimes snuggle into bed when one or both of us needs that human connection. It's not sexual with him—it goes so much deeper than that. A pure platonic love I treasure.

Angel isn't the only friend with benefits to have shared my bed. And plenty of my other hookups have asked me for legal advice. Enough that I tend not to share my profession with one-offs anymore. That's part of why I don't mind helping Angel; they don't *expect* me to give them my expertise as a perk of sleeping together.

"Thanks, Saint."

"You're welcome, darling." I pat their hands. "I'm loathe to chase you out of my bed, but you should probably go before Owen wonders where you are."

"Shit." They glance at the clock and bite their lip. "Yeah. Next week?"

"I'll be waiting. Will you be kid free next weekend?"

"Probably not? Trevor already said he's going out of town. I've got the texts saved."

That shouldn't be so disappointing. And I'll still have them to myself in a week. I can wait a week to kiss them and come with them.

"Right, well, try to get some rest?"

"Yeah. With all my free time." They laugh as they pull on their pants. "I'll stay awake next time. You don't have to walk me out."

They leave before I can protest. That isn't what I meant. Maybe it's better to leave things as they stand. Let them pull away slowly instead of drawing them into complicated, messy feelings. I like them too much to let them think I resent the lack of sex, though, so I text them.

Saint: I had a nice nap with you. Thanks for spending your free time with me tonight.

I add and delete a heart emoji. That might come on too strong. Angel sends back a thumbs up. Well, they're in a rush to get their kid. I shouldn't expect a wall of text or anything.

Saint: You're an amazing parent and you're doing the best you can.

Angel: I guess. Doesn't ever feel like enough for anyone.

I type: *you're exactly right for me.* Stare at it. Delete the message. Type it again, in half a dozen reworded permutations. I settle on sending something more innocuous.

Saint: I'm sure your kids would tell you that you're plenty.

The only reply I get to that is a laugh react, but Angel's got to be driving, so I try not to read into their silence.

I care about Angel. As a friend, and as someone who I really enjoy fucking. That might look a lot like romance, but it doesn't change the core of who I am, and I don't want it to. Even with Carl, I've never had the sort of swoony squishes he gets on every new romantic interest. That internal giddy drive to pursue someone specific to be with them.

It just gets complicated because I enjoy sex and it's even better with someone I like to be around after we both come. Much like how movies are better with friends. I love my friends, and I try to bring as much to my friendships as I take from them. Angel is just becoming a *really* good friend, and most people don't take it well if I reciprocate a romantic love declaration with caveats and declarations of undying friendship.

So when Carl gets home from running bingo night for his senior citizen charity, I'm waiting for him. I bring a bottle of wine I meant to share with Angel in the afterglow over to my bestie's place. Carl will distract me from the growing emotions I'm not ready to face.

❧ ❧

CARL GRINS WHEN HE catches sight of me lurking outside his door when he gets back from his bingo night. Days of Grace is the elder care charity he started and now runs. It's his dream job, but the sweet bear of a man is also genuinely friends with most of his clients. His smile falls as his gaze flicks from my face to the bottle of wine cradled against my chest.

"You okay?"

"Oh. Yeah. It's nothing. I just wanted some company to share this with." I hold the bottle aloft.

Carl doesn't bother checking the label since I'm the wine snob between the two of us. He likes his wine as sweet as he is and he trusts me to take his palate into account when I buy for us. He steps past me, pulling out his keys to let us into his half of our duplex.

The side by side two-story units share a mirrored layout, but we have very different styles. His place is a riot of bright colors and warm textures. Throw blankets on his overstuffed couch, a braided rag rug in the entryway, that sort of thing. He'll change up the decor seasonally too, the big sap.

My place is elegant neutrals that looked nice in the showroom. Carl calls it austere, but I like things simple. I made sure the seating was comfortable and then sort of left it as a blank canvas. Not like I'm leaving room for a partner's personal touches. I have no plans to share my space with someone as vibrant as Carl again some day.

Except the more Angel keeps coming around, the more I could maybe envision them leaving their mark on all my pristine neutrals. Which is absurd. The thought even crossing my mind should be a flashing neon exit sign to end this thing that's been going on between us for the past while. With anyone else, it would be. But Angel is safe, because they don't have the time to pick out throw pillows or paint my walls or whatever else.

We make a quick detour through the kitchen for a bottle opener and two stemless wine goblets. In contrast to my home's starkness, Carl already has plenty of his own home decor. As evidenced by the fact he has to toss dainty throw pillows onto the floor to make room for us on the couch.

"Is that why they call them throw pillows?" I muse.

"Huh? You lost me, babe." Carl reaches for the wine bottle. I hand it over so he can open it for us.

"You know." I gesture at the pillows now littering his cushy area rug. "Because you throw them on the ground to actually use the furniture."

Carl tsks at me. "Just because your home sense is inspired by Stay-Puft..."

"It's not!" I shove at him. Although he's not entirely wrong, shades of marshmallow would describe my home's color palette. Sure, it can be a pain to keep it clean, but it looks nice as long as I keep up with my housework and it's not like I have kids or pets around to stain the upholstery.

"Hey, watch the wine," Carl warns as he pours us each a glass.

I take mine and sip from it. "Mm, it's good."

Carl does likewise, and we both savor the wine for a moment, sitting side by side to unwind after a long day. It's almost like when we were married, but without the fraught expectations that tore us apart. I don't want to think about what we can't have. Better to bask in what we do share.

"I have style." I set my glass on a coaster and flop dramatically across Carl's lap. He curls his knees up to prop his feet on the table and cradle me there. Then he runs his fingers through my hair. I've come to accept the premature graying and I like that Carl calls it distinguished.

Carl gives me all the sweet affection I can't let myself have with anyone else without sending mixed signals. We might not fit together in any traditional relationship sense or in bed, but cuddling on his couch I feel utterly content. With Carl, it's safe to let my guard down and love with all of myself.

"Uh huh, I bet I'm going to have to drag you away from the sad beige baby aisle when we go shopping for Gail and Marcus's baby shower." Carl is smiling down at me and for a brief second, I miss the days when I could kiss that smile, but it's a fleeting thought. We don't kiss because it means very different things to Carl than it does to me and we don't work that way.

"Sad beige babies?" I repeat, teasing him.

"Yeah, it's a whole thing. Gail's been sending me nursery inspo since she found out about the baby. You seriously haven't seen the hashtag?"

"Um, no, because babies are sticky little monsters and I don't hang out on parenting TikTok or wherever you find that crap." I wave away Carl's assumptions that I would know anything about parenting hashtags.

It's not like I hate children. I just don't spend time with them outside of Carl's niece. And probably this new nibling of his once they're born. I've seen Angel's kids at Carl's family gatherings since they're Marcus's niblings. I'm sure they're great, but I am not crossing the kinds of lines with Angel it would take to become involved in their kids' lives. And I keep circling back to thoughts of them when I came here not to worry about what we're doing and the messages I'm sending.

"They're cute." Carl points out. "And the hashtag is pretty funny. You'd be totally into a sad beige nursery."

"Uh, huh? How does a sad beige baby even sound?"

Carl scrunches up his face in a ridiculous imitation of a bawling baby. "You know, sad."

I can't suppress my grin at that. I let out a guffaw and pat at his bushy, bearded cheek in a conciliatory gesture. "Don't quit your day job to become an actor, babe. That was awful."

"Well, I wouldn't try out for a baby role."

"Are baby rolls like lobster rolls?"

"No, baby rolls are their cute little chubby rolls of totally pinchable fat."

"Gotcha, so you like to pinch and eat babies." I nod sagely at him. As though I'm not being totally ridiculous. I have to bite my cheek to keep a straight face.

"No." Carl swats at my chest. "I didn't say any of that. You are a menace."

"You totally did. I'm telling Gail."

Carl rolls his eyes at me. "You can't distract me forever. What had you so sad on my doorstep?"

"Nothing. I just wanted company tonight." And if I have a twinge of wishing that company was the sweet little snack who fell asleep with my mouth on their bits earlier and slept in my arms like I was the safest place on the planet, well, that doesn't take anything away from the way I feel about Carl.

My love for him is as steady and true as the tides ebbing and flowing through every season of our lives. Whatever delusions I have about a future with Angel will pass. They'll have to when Angel is ready to move on because they have time to pursue someone who can be everything they need and deserve. I'll bow out gracefully when that day comes, the same as I will when Carl finds the man who will sweep him off his feet. And in the meantime, I'll enjoy what I have with each of them for as long as it lasts.

Carl draws me out of my maudlin thoughts with his fingers massaging my scalp. "I am always down to cuddle; you know that isn't ever going to change, right?"

"I do," I lie through my teeth with a tight smile and then I change the subject. "Tell me about bingo night? Or are there any new prospects for getting me out of those pesky alimony payments?"

Our divorce was entirely amicable. There is no court-ordered alimony between us, even though he supported me through law school. So I've always made sure he's taken care of, despite his occasional protests.

I invested in getting his non-profit off the ground. I made sure he could afford his share of the mortgage when we bought this place so we could always live close together and be involved in each other's lives. And I put aside alimony payments for him every month because I always want him to be financially secure.

He's still my life partner, even if he isn't my romantic partner or lover. And teasing him about getting out of those payments is my way of telling him I support his search for the next great love of his life.

Carl gives me a searching look. He's wise to all my tricks; that's the problem with loving your best friend. But he doesn't call me on my bullshit, and I enjoy hearing about his day and a guy he's been flirting with online. We snuggle and share another glass of wine each while we chat. I end up sleeping over at his place, both of us fully clothed under his homey quilt and a downy duvet. It's totally platonic, and exactly what I need to ground me.

Chapter 4

ANGEL (OCTOBER 9TH, 2023)

THE DINER IS SLAMMED for brunch on Saturday. It's been so long since I worked a weekend shift, I've almost forgotten how busy we get. Although the fact it's our Thanksgiving weekend probably plays a role, too. The tips are wild at least. Until they aren't.

It's almost refreshing to be so run off my feet there's no room for stressing about anything except keeping my customers happy. No time to check my phone for grumpy texts from Meg. I'm sure she's been complaining that Grandma wants to actually spend time together instead of letting her hide on her phone and text her friends.

No pining over an alternate universe where I could stay in bed with Saint for hours, making lazy love to him all night long. No mentally tallying the assignments I need to finish if I want to pass the last two classes that I need to start my fourteen weeks of practicum experience. I'm so close to crossing the last hurdle to getting my teaching certification.

Between the kids and just life, sometimes it feels like I've been in school forever, watching my classmates get younger year after year as I struggle through my coursework as time and finances have allowed. I started this degree when I was still with Trevor, he badgered me about wasting the time and money on an education I didn't need, but it's something I really want and now my dreams are within reach. Things will get better soon.

None of that matters right now though. Just feeding hungry people with food that I don't have to cook on dishes that I only rarely have to wash. Though, with Josie and Raul calling in sick, we all have to pitch in to cover the slack. Several customers come in to pick up pie orders for the holiday on Monday. So that's an added complication we don't deal with most weekends, but it's all routine after doing this job since I was pregnant with Meg.

It takes me aback when Trevor and his mom come in for lunch with the kids. Elk's Pass might be a small town, but this is far from the only brunch option. I try to catch Amy's eye to not seat them in my section, but Trevor points to a booth. Amy nods, leading the way with a stack of menus, and my fate is sealed. I grit my teeth and welcome them with the usual spiel.

I can't blame Amy. She's a new hire and I have the kids in often enough that everyone knows them. Of course she wouldn't realize I don't want to serve my ex when he's here with them.

If it was anyone else, that would be fine. But the way Trevor smirks at me as he places his order is like razors made of ice under my skin. Ice, because they melt away without leaving a trace for anyone else to notice while I'm bleeding on the inside.

It's in the little things. His sneering *thank you, ma'am.* The way his eyes scrape my body raw when he looks at me, never focusing on my face when he could ogle my chest or ass. His dismissiveness of me and our kids when he tells Owen to, "Speak up, she can't hear you when you mumble, son."

Or when he tells Meg, "put your damned phone away or you'll lose it. Can't you see your mom's annoyed with you? There's nowhere to put your plate."

"It's fine, hun." I slide the plate in front of my daughter as she shoots daggers at Trevor with her eyes. If he takes her phone away, I can't afford to replace it again. Damnation.

I should expect it when he has his mom leave first with the kids. But we're busy as fuck. I just got a twelve-top with two babies in high chairs, a bar order big enough to drown a moose, and a severe dairy allergy. So I don't notice Trevor skipping out on the bill until he's long gone.

When I get to the empty table, I just stare at the crayon scrawled note he left on a napkin. I bite my cheek to hold back my angry tears.

Thanks for the meal, Angie.

I crumple the note into a ball and bite back a scream. I'm not sure if the feminine nickname is better or worse than my actual deadname. Fuck him. Fuck, fuck fuck. I can't catch my breath as I stare at the empty plates and try to tally up the cost in my head.

Someone touches my arm, and I flinch. Amy looks at me with wide, apologetic eyes. "Did you not want me to put your family in your section?"

"Trevor's my ex. So, yeah, please don't the next time he's with my kids."

"Oh. Is something wrong?" Amy shifts uncomfortably.

I can't stop the hysterical laughter that bubbles out of me. "No, not at all. He just ducked out on the bill."

"Shit, I can try to catch him?" Amy glances out the window, but it's too late for that. From her uncertain tone, it's an empty offer regardless.

"Don't bother." I wave her back to her post. "There are people waiting to be seated and we're slammed."

"Yeah. That's actually what I wanted to ask you. The guys who just came in requested you. You want them? You seemed stressed, so I wanted to check in about the request, in case... Might make up for the bad cheque; they're dressed nice." Amy rubs her fingers together to indicate they have money.

I glance warily over; I'm so not in the mood to flirt for a tip right now. My femme presentation for work—long hair styled into bouncy waves, just enough makeup to all but erase the gradual facial changes from T, and a flowy blouse that obscures my figure—tends to net me better tips than when I lean into my more masculine attributes.

I'm okay with both sides of that particular coin these days. Not being forced into femininity by my circumstances anymore makes it easier to embrace the parts I still relate with. Even if dressing feminine at work all but forces me to paste on a smile for the customers and exposes me to more harassment.

I follow Amy's line of sight to where Carl Meadows is standing near the door. He waves to me when he notices me looking. I wave back, breathing a sigh of relief.

"Yeah, seat him in my section. That's fine." I won't have to pretend for Saint's ex-husband. Technically, Carl is practically my brother-in-law, in the sense that he's at all the same family gatherings I'm invited to, since our siblings are married. But the connection to Saint feels more immediate. Maybe because my brother and I aren't close. Not estranged, like I am with our parents. But I'm too busy to reconnect with the brother who was too involved with his own life to help me when I was alone in the world.

That's not entirely fair. He was in Toronto for university when I fucked up my life, too far away to be aware of my drama and in no position to intervene. Not like I could have spent Meg's baby years crashing in Marcus's dorm room.

Regardless, it's the connection to Saint that makes me smile at Carl. I spent last night wrapped up in Saint's arms since the kids were with Trevor. The memory of that is so comforting, I can almost imagine his woodsy cologne enveloping me in a bubble of safety. A haven set apart from all my vying responsibilities.

It's not my imagination when his hand lands on my shoulder. His voice is a warm buzz in my ear. "What's the matter, darling?"

"Nothing," I mumble, turning to face Saint and wishing I could just give in to the urge to sob on his shoulder about everything. He's searching my expression, and I get the impression he isn't quite up to having me fling myself into his arms. It's enough for him to be standing there, ready to offer a listening ear. The hand on my shoulder slips down to pat my back. I give myself to the count of ten to savor his comforting touch while I get myself under control.

Saint doesn't pry.

But Amy can't keep her mouth shut. "Her ex pulled a dine and dash."

"*Their* ex," Saint clips out the correction.

I don't have the energy to care about one more little dig under my skin. I'd care more if Amy wasn't so new, and the most forgetful person on staff. She doesn't use the wrong pronouns out of malice.

"Right. Sorry, Angel." Amy smiles apologetically at me. "I'll work on that."

"Don't worry about it." I scrub at my eyes and wave her over to the hostess station where the line of waiting guests is getting restless. "Just go deal with all of that."

"On it." Amy grimaces, then plasters on her customer service face and goes to manage the crowd.

"You all right?" Saint checks.

"Yeah." I allow myself one last sniffle, then take a deep breath to collect myself before I step out of Saint's arms, uncomfortable with the concern in his eyes. "I'm fine."

"Mhm." It's clear he isn't buying it.

"I am," I protest. Maybe if I argue hard enough, I can convince myself. Too bad he's better at verbal sparring than I'll ever be.

"Liar."

I stick my tongue out at him, and he lifts a brow at me.

"Behave," he says in his sexy *I mean business* rumble that has Bitsy perking up. Pavlovian response.

I bite my lip and stifle my needy little whine. "For you? Always."

"Good, darling." Saint's eyes twinkle, those gorgeous laugh lines around them crinkle, and for a minute I'm sure he's going to kiss me. Right here in front of Carl and the entire packed diner. But he just pats my cheek and leaves me to bus my table with inhuman speed. I need to grab another round of drink orders for my crankily indecisive party of twelve and put in kid's meal orders for them.

It's a relief when Amy manages to find a clear table and seats Carl and Saint in my section. I almost burst into grateful tears when they tell me they aren't in any hurry and to take my time with their orders. I check in on them as much as I can. When they colossally overtip me for crappy service, I feel like shit for letting them be my lowest priority in the midst of the lunchtime rush. They must have realized I'd object because they leave the money tucked under their empty glasses instead of giving me the opportunity to refuse their charity.

My pride wars with the unpaid receipt for Trevor's meal. Not to mention the five-dollar tip that my party of twelve left on their massive split check bill with a ridiculous bar tab. I pocket the cash. I still have to tip the bar staff proportionate to their work, regardless of my party cheaping out on me.

One of the dinner staff calls out, so I get pressed into working a double. I need the extra hours, so I don't complain. I get half an hour between lunch and dinner service to buy myself a discounted meal and scarf it down in the corner of the bar.

At the end of the night, I'm dreading settling up with everyone. I have to tip out the hostesses and bar staff. Amy already took her share and left ages ago, but her evening shift replacement gets a cut too. My manager gives me a confused frown over Trevor's unpaid bill and waves away my math.

"What are you talking about? Your other table asked to cover your kids' meals."

"Huh?" But I know exactly who covered for Trevor's nonsense. Saint. For someone who insists he doesn't do relationships, he sure has a funny way of showing it.

"It's covered. Don't worry about it, Angel. Finish your side work and go home."

I clamp my mouth shut on any further objections. As I finish tidying, I ignore everyone around me. I'm not getting paid enough to chit chat. Heck, since we're supposed to do side work off the clock, I'm not getting paid at all.

Still, it could be worse. Thanks to Saint and Carl, I might actually make money off this shift instead of barely breaking even after all of today's fuckery.

I'm exhausted from the double shift and the busy weekend crowds when I finally leave the diner. It's dark and I'm exhausted and emotional. So it's no wonder my heart leaps into my throat, pulse pounding a million kilometers an hour, at someone calling my name across the poorly lit parking lot. It doesn't stop pounding when I see who's waving me over, though for entirely different reasons.

Saint.

"What are you doing here?"

Saint shrugs. "You told me when your shift ends, remember?"

"So? I'm not really up for a fuck tonight. I was going to text you from my bubble bath to cancel."

"Last I checked, friends with benefits are still a type of friend. Friends check on each other after a bad day."

"I told you I was fine. You didn't have to swoop in and save me. I'm not your good deed." I don't want his pity in bed or out of it, though I'm not tired enough to spew that last bit at him mere steps from my workplace.

The idea he might see me as a charity case is like ice in my veins. I shiver. But that's not really fair; he's never given me a reason to think that.

Saint is just generous to a fault and a gesture that seems huge to me is probably pocket change to him. Thinking back to the sliding scale rate that he charged me for his legal services, yeah. My entire shoestring budget is roughly what he spends on those shiny loafers of his. Or the tailored suits I love seeing on his floor almost as much as on his body.

I'm in a bad mood, dead on my feet. I miss my kids, and I'm going to say or do something I regret if I stay here, so I turn toward my car. Saint grabs my wrist.

My pulse thunders loud enough to drown out the sounds of cars on the nearby road, and I tense for whatever happens next. The pain of a crushing grip trying to force me into compliance doesn't come. Saint just holds me gently in place. The second I jerk my arm away, he lets me go, holding up his hands defensively. I'm so tired.

"What do you want?" I whisper.

"Just to make sure you're okay."

"Well, I'm not."

"I can see that. Want to come over and watch movies?"

I snort. "You aren't going to offer to run me a bubble bath and massage my aching feet?"

"Do you want me to offer you that?" His lips quirk up into an almost smile.

"No. You made it pretty clear you don't do the whole boyfriend thing." The bitter words slip out before I can stop myself or think them through. They hit like a sucker punch and Saint's wry smile slips from his face like it was never there. His shoulders—so strong they always seem up to carrying any burden—slump. Shit. I hurt him.

I stare at him wide-eyed, wishing I could take it back. That isn't even what I want from him, so why throw it in his face? But I know why. He's too perfect and I need to remind myself that this isn't going to end with him sweeping me off my feet like some sort of fairy tale.

"I don't do romance," Saint murmurs, voice carefully measured. "But I can absolutely take care of you if you spell out what you need from me as a person who cares about you."

"And not a person who just wants in my pants?" I could kick myself for shoving away the best offer I'm going to get for someone to at least go through the motions of taking care of me. It's like my mouth has a mind of its own. But somehow, I must hit the right balance between acerbic and teasing.

"Angel, darling, don't take this the wrong way, but I hardly need to sweep you off your feet for that." Saint smiles again, hurt, but still holding out the metaphorical hand of friendship. I want to clasp it and never let go.

"Ouch, right in the feels." I press a hand to my heart in a dramatic gesture to mask just how close to old wounds his words hit, like I hurt him. Insults hurled at me in anger. I'm allowed to enjoy sex. I am. And he's allowed to set his own boundaries.

"Sorry, did that hit a nerve?" Saint asks, with so much sincerity I'm guilty all over again for my remarks about him.

I nod. He reaches for me again, gently rubbing his thumb along my jaw.

"Ah, my bad. I like that you enjoy sex, Angel. I enjoy it too. Nothing wrong with that. Just don't expect me to come up with all that lovey-dovey grand gesture stuff on my own. Carl's the one who said you might need some TLC tonight. He's the one you want if you're into that romance shit." Saint tries to make that sound exasperated, but his voice and his smile both go all soft. Those warm crinkles around his eyes deepen when he talks about Carl. Love. That's what it looks like when someone really loves another person.

It's not something I can have. I blew my chances at that sort of sweeping love story when I thought I could have it with Trevor. Well, I might not get romance, but I got my kids out of all my terrible life choices.

They're completely worth everything. Even if I'm struggling to keep the food in their bellies and a roof over their heads. And that reminds me that Owen needs new shoes for tae kwon do and Meg is going to need to order dance recital costumes soon.

Fingers crossed it's a color that won't require buying new shoes to match. Or DIYing a dye job. Last time my fingers were a weird shade of gangrenous chartreuse for weeks and I'm convinced it didn't do my tips any favors. I don't have time to wallow in self-pity. But I could use a friend.

"I'm sorry too. You're a good friend, Saint. What movie were you thinking?"

"Have you seen *Rising Storm?*" Saint's face lights up with excitement. "It's that new superhero flick set in Toronto."

"Sure, so long as I don't have to follow a complex plot, I'm down for pretty special effects."

"Perfect. You can take that bubble bath while I make popcorn, if you want?"

"That sounds really nice, Saint. Thanks."

"I'll meet you at my place, then." He smiles at me, melting the ice around my heart that little bit more as he turns toward his car.

Chapter 5

ANGEL (DECEMBER 1ST, 2023)

"YOUR MUSIC SUCKS, POP." Meg scrolls through my phone looking for music to play. It's a rare Friday night where all three of us are home with no activities to distract from our family time.

She's been using my phone since Trevor confiscated hers. So far, he's refusing all my efforts to get it back. I'm still holding out hope I can reason with him. If not, replacing it is going to put a severe damper on my holiday shopping budget, but I'm not dwelling on that. Tonight, I am going to enjoy my time with my kids.

"Play Mariah," Owen suggests as he sorts through the tangled ball of Christmas lights to get it ready for the tree. He has to push the floppy end of his green and red sequined elf hat out of his face. He still loves the goofy hat he got for a long-ago holiday themed dress-up day at school. It was the first thing he dug out of the box of decorations. "Bring on all the Christmas!" He throws up excited jazz hands that make Meg roll her eyes and sigh dramatically as she cues up his song request.

"Fine, I guess I can stream her."

I open up the battered tree box. The kids and I always put up our Christmas tree on December first. It's probably stupid to cling to my mom's traditions years after she turned her back on me, but it gives the holidays some structure. That's something I sorely need to get me through this season without breaking.

At least the upbeat music isn't as depressing as some of the carols the kids could have picked. My family's farm grows more than Christmas trees, but the fact we sold trees always meant Christmas was a big deal before I was cast out. Those memories are tarnished, but I still try to give my kids all the holiday magic I'm too jaded to feel anymore.

Saint and Carl's duplex has been dripping with holiday lights for the better part of a month now, which he says is Carl's doing. I know what a sap Saint is for the people he cares about though, so I'm certain he was right in the thick of things stringing them up.

Although, when I was there last night, Saint still didn't have his tree up yet. I can't help wondering what his tree trimming traditions are. Probably something with Carl. The thought of Saint smiling indulgently as Carl prods him into decorating makes me smile too.

Saint's tree last year was a magazine-worthy confection of sparkling gold and silver tinsel and baubles. It was gorgeous, but didn't reflect any of Saint's sweet playfulness. Beautiful, but soulless compared to all the love packed into my family's hodge-podge of memories.

Our scraggly artificial tree is older than Meg. It looks worse for wear when I dig it out of storage. Even so, it's what we always use. Always. Trevor's mom got it for us the Christmas I was pregnant with Meg.

I was still living in her finished basement and my own little tree was the first thing that made me feel like everything might be okay. She sat beside me by the light of this tree while the two of us stumbled through knitting the lumpy squares of a baby blanket for Meg. The blanket—and Trevor's mom—gave me the permission I needed to fall in love with my baby. This tree gave me hope for our future.

So it might be small and ugly, but I get it assembled and fluff out the branches to make it look fuller with all the devotion of a ritual. Meg sorts idly through our box of ornaments as she texts her friends under the pretense of curating the playlist. I'm on to her tricks, but I'm just glad she's making at least the token effort of spending time with us.

I'm so unbelievably proud of my daughter. She's fiercely independent to the point I don't really worry about her doing the sort of stupid things I did at her age seeking acceptance and my peer's approval. It probably helps that she has an amazing group of close friends.

She's cooler than I'll ever be. Even though most of her wardrobe is thrifted, she wears her vintage apparel with poise. My eldest has all of Trevor's acerbic wit and the humor that first drew me to him with almost none of his meanness. She's brilliant and funny and heartbreakingly responsible.

It's a lifesaver when she helps with Owen's homework and getting ready for school. My heart wants to burst with pride, but my guilt can be overwhelming. For all that they have their moments of sibling rivalry, she adores her baby brother. I do my best not to put too much on her young shoulders.

I still wish I could be around more so Meg wouldn't feel like she needs to take on so much. So many people have rolled their eyes at me for refusing to treat her like a built-in babysitter for her brother. But not making Owen her responsibility unless Meg is willing and fairly compensated isn't negotiable for me.

"Here, you'll like this one, Owen." Meg plays another song.

"Oh, yes! Turn it up?" Owen sings along.

Meg smiles indulgently at him as she turns up the holiday music. She watches him dancing in place—his elf hat in danger of flopping right off his head—as he continues to untangle the lights.

They never fail to brighten my mood when they're being silly together like this. That assuages my guilt over Meg having to grow up so fast. Family helps each other. I couldn't have asked for two better kids. Meg calls me on my bullshit, practical to a fault. Owen, my sweet little goober, has been a ray of pure sunshine from the moment I first brought him home. He was the smiliest baby I've ever met, and he somehow hasn't outgrown that cheerfulness.

"Ready for the lights, Pop?" Owen holds up the glowing strand. The kid's nimble fingers somehow have the entire tangled mess sorted out in the time it took me to assemble the tree. Even though he was bopping along to Meg's playlist the entire time.

"Just about." I adjust the top few branches and reach for the lights. "Alright, let's get this place lit."

"Yes! Wait, *lit* like lighting all the tree lights, or like how Meg uses it?" Owen glances earnestly between us.

"Lit isn't a thing anymore," Meg informs me. Or maybe both of us, because Owen nods.

"No cap?" I tease her.

"Pop!" Meg groans. "No. Just because you want to teach the youth doesn't mean you get to try speaking like us."

"Yeah, Pop. It sounds weird when you try to talk like Meg," Owen adds as he scrambles to his feet. He promptly trips over the strand of lights he's trying to hand me, all gawky limbs from growing another inch in the past month. How are they both growing up so damn fast?

It's like I'm watching the scene unfold in slow motion as he stumbles to correct the fall and lurches right into the damn tree. I grab for his shoulders, holding him up as the tree goes crashing to the ground. It takes everything in me not to burst into tears at the sharp crack of breaking plastic as two of the four legs snap off the base.

"Oopsy?" Owen gazes up at me wide-eyed. Holding him close, I can feel his heart pounding in his chest.

I swallow down my hurt frustration about the tree breaking. At least my kid is okay. He's going to feel bad enough without me piling my emotions onto his narrow shoulders. I take a deep, steadying breath, rubbing his arms and counting until the worst of the impotent anger at the unfairness of it all passes.

"You're just brimming with grace lately," Meg observes, giving Owen tacit permission to shrug off what just happened.

"Tada!" He throws up more of those jazz hands and tries to play it off like a joke, defusing the tension in the way he's so damn good at. He shouldn't have to do that, but the kid loves to make people laugh. He's a natural performer and I'm probably going to be cheering him on at every show once he's old enough to try out for the high school's theater group. The tree was important to me, sure, but he could break a thousand trees and it wouldn't change a thing about how much I adore him.

Meg snorts and shakes her head at her brother's antics.

"Are you okay?" I check, holding him at arm's length and ignoring Meg's commentary.

"Yeah. I'm tougher than I look," he grumbles, like it's a sore spot. He's smaller than most of his peers since his birthday falls right before the age cutoff, making him the youngest kid in his class. Inheriting my short stature doesn't help. He hasn't been as self-conscious about his size since starting tae kwon do though. The martial arts lessons have done wonders for his confidence. But I guess even at ten, those insecurities die hard.

"I know you're tough, kiddo." I ruffle his hair. Then I turn to the wreckage of our tree and make a fruitless effort to get it to stand on the two remaining legs still attached to the base. Eventually, I have to concede there's no salvaging the broken base. "I guess we aren't decorating tonight. Sorry, guys."

Owen's face falls. "I'm sorry, Pop." His hands flutter at his sides, like he's itching to make it better when he knows he can't.

"Want me to call Uncle Marcus about getting a tree from the farm?" Meg holds up my phone.

No. That's a terrible idea for so many reasons. I don't want a real tree that smells like a home I can never go back to, or for my kid to call and fix my problems. I especially don't want my brother to think we need his charity. Most of all, I don't want Meg to have to beg for gifts I'm too proud to accept and too broke to give her.

"I can call him." I hold out my hand for the phone. Meg rolls her eyes as she slaps the phone into my palm. Marcus answers on the second ring.

"Hey, sis—sib." He corrects the slip of his tongue in a rush, and it's fine. He's trying. "Sorry about that. How's it going? Did the kids finally convince you to go with a real tree this year? I've got a load all ready to

ALEX SILVER

take to the holiday market. Just say the word and I can swing by your place with one tonight."

Of course he offers to deliver a tree to us before I can even tell him that's why I'm calling.

"Uh, yeah. Turns out ours is broken," I admit. "Are you sure though? I can't pay you until next week. After payday."

Marcus tuts at me. "It's our family's farm, Angel. Everyone in the family gets their first tree for the year free. I'm not taking your money as long as I'm in charge. End of discussion."

He is the one in charge since our parents retired and spend their winters in sunnier climes these days. I bet Carl and Saint's trees are from the farm too. I can cope with the pine smell and the needles. It was kind of nostalgic in Saint's living room last year. Although that was in smaller doses than taking care of a tree of my own. I'll just have to deal with it. For the kids.

"Are you sure?" I bite my lip, wanting to insist. I don't really want any piece of my parents' legacy anymore, even if it comes from my brother. Marcus wasn't around when everything came crashing down for me. He had nothing to do with it. But he wasn't there for me back then either, and part of me can't help resenting that absence.

"Do you know how many trees I've brought to Gail's sister's house for her annual holiday party? My sibling gets the same treatment," Marcus insists. I suppose it makes sense that he'd treat me the same as his wife's siblings.

"Okay. Thank you."

"We'll need a stand too," Meg pipes up in the background, loud enough for Marcus to overhear her.

He chuckles. "Tell my niece I'll be there with everything you need to get it set up in about an hour, and tell both kids *hi* for me?"

"Here, I'll just put you on speaker so you can tell them yourself. They're both right here."

"Hey, kids," Marcus says.

"Hi, Uncle Marcus," Owen waves at the phone, even though it's not a video call.

"Excited for your first real tree?" Marcus asks.

"Yes! They smell so good, like Christmas and happiness!" Owen bounces on his toes, repeating a line I know he has to have gotten from my brother.

"That's right." Marcus chuckles. "Nothing quite like a real tree to Make the Yuletide Gay."

Owen beams. "Like that old song?"

"Sure, kiddo," Marcus agrees.

"That fits, since our tree is already pretty gay." Meg lifts our collection of pride ornaments out of the box to emphasize her point.

She made me the pink, blue, and white painted trans pride ornament the year I came out to her. It's just a painted ball, but I like the colors better than the nonbinary one that also fits me, and I love that she made it for me. She was only a little older than Owen is now. She came out to me last year by presenting me with the enamel pink, blue, and lavender bisexual pride cat ornament.

After that, Owen asked if he gets a flag too. So we hung a jolly roger for him because Meg reminded him of the two years he had to wear a patch for his amblyopia. The only thing that made him keep it on was their running joke that it made him a pirate.

Those three ornaments mean the world to me. A visual symbol that our love for each other is unconditional, the way family should always be. The way it wasn't for me. That thought makes it hard to talk to Marcus like everything is fine.

I hand the phone back to Meg and start disassembling the broken tree as an excuse to step back from the conversation my kids are having with Marcus. They discuss the relative merits of white versus rainbow holiday lights. I need to clear space for the tree my brother is bringing to replace ours. Seeing my son so animated about his first real tree takes the sting out of having to say goodbye to our old one.

Maybe it will be better to let go of the memories that cling to these flimsy branches. We'll still have all the ornaments that represent the good times. We can make new memories and traditions if I let go of the past represented by the dusty box holding the broken remnants of our old tree.

I want to freeze frame Owen's round cheeks and bright cherubic smile as he gesticulates to emphasize his words. He pouts theatrically at his sister's gentle teasing over his taste in music. Marcus talks to my kids for a while longer. I can't hold the past against him too much when he's being a good uncle, giving them the Christmas they deserve.

I try to pack away my heartache along with the old tree so we can focus on having a good time decorating our new tree once it arrives. My brother is so cheery with my kids as he helps get it set up and level. Gail even sends over a little tupperware full of holiday trail mix with the tree delivery. Her 'puppy chow' is basically just chocolate, peanut butter, and powdered sugar on cereal, but Owen loves it.

It's easier to focus on enjoying the moment when Owen drags Meg into twirling around the tree with him. The two of them work together to thread the lights onto its bushy boughs as they dance. My heart swells with love for the two of them. We work together to put our memories on the new tree, and I can't help smiling at how happy they both are to draw out the family tradition. The three of us sit close on our tiny couch to bask in the sense of accomplishment—and the lights—when it's done. I snap a picture to share with Saint later, certain the bright colors will make him smile.

"Movie night?" Owen asks, digging into Gail's cereal treats. Meg grabs a fistful of the sweets, and I even pick at the snack.

"I'm up for some *Elf*." Meg pulls up a streaming service on the phone, using a friend's login information and casting the movie to our television. Ugh. I shouldn't feel guilty that I can't afford every streaming service under the sun. It's not like the kids have any shortage of media to consume.

Owen shrugs in under my arm and snuggles into my side, distracting me from my self-recriminations and just filling me with love for him. Once the movie starts, Meg drops her head onto my shoulder on my other side. She even puts away her phone to watch the holiday classic with us.

These are the moments when I think I'm doing alright, the three of us together and making memories. I love my kids so much it scares me sometimes. They deserve so much more than I have a blueprint to give them, but I must be doing something right. How many kids their ages want to spend Friday night watching movies with their parent instead of out with their friends or doing their own things in their rooms?

I'm going to give my kids a Christmas season to remember. More nights like this, with the three of us together. More songs, snacks, and holding each other close. We all laugh at Buddy's holiday antics, and I know in my heart that I'm enough for them.

Even if I can't put the latest tech under the tree, I can give them these moments of togetherness to treasure. They will never doubt how much they're both adored.

Chapter 6

Saint (December 13th, 2023)

"It's snowing!" Carl twirls around in the season's first dusting of the stuff, grinning like a little kid as we leave the gym. We try to go together at least three times a week, one of those routine set points that helps us stay connected in the midst of our busy lives.

"Damn, it's cold," I complain, but I can't help smiling at his enjoyment. The snow glistens as it catches in his bushy beard and melts there.

"Spoilsport." Carl doesn't look at me, just sticks out his tongue to catch the fluffy flakes, the big adorable goofball. "I've got a date tonight."

"Same guy you've been chatting with online?" I ask, trying to keep my voice normal. I have to turn away, heart aching with how much I want him to have everything that makes him happy. For Carl to have the romance he craves, I might have to give him more space, but I'd do anything for him.

"Yeah. He says he's fine with taking things slow." Carl shoves his hands into his pockets.

"That's good." I amble toward our cars.

"Yep. So, I can't do dinner with you tonight." Carl trails after me.

"That's fine." I snug my jacket more firmly around me. Time to break out my scarf and gloves when I get home. I spare a brief thought to whether Angel's kids have all the winter gear they need. Knowing my friend, almost definitely. Whether Angel has warm things too is another issue entirely.

"Come over for a shake and help me pick an outfit?" Carl breaks into my thoughts.

"Oh, so now you like my sad beige style?" I tease, arching a brow at him. We both know my wardrobe is on point. My suits sort of have to be when I need to appear in court. Appearances matter with clients and judges alike. And I appreciate nice clothes. My big bear of a best friend is too broad to fit most of my clothing, but I can still help him pick something from his own closet.

Carl pouts at me. "I mean, neutrals work for an adult date look. I want him to take me seriously."

"You look good in bright colors, babe." I bump our shoulders together as we walk toward our cars. "Don't let anyone take your joy, yeah?"

"I won't," he says defensively. Carl plucks self-consciously at the bright pink joggers he's wearing home from the gym. His nerves have me questioning whether he's just that eager to make things work. Or if it's more likely this guy isn't actually as good a fit as Carl hopes he is.

"Meet you at home?" I suggest. Only time will tell if the guy is a jerk. I'll be there to support Carl either way.

"Sure." We each get into our cars and he follows me out of the parking lot.

It's Wednesday. A week since my last hit of happiness with Angel. One day shy of my favorite routine lately. Not that I don't still love my time with Carl, but Angel fulfills different needs. One more night alone before I get to taste the sweetest lips.

Angel will be busy with the kids right now, but I want to pull out my phone to confirm tomorrow. I bet Owen is bouncing off the walls, anticipating the upcoming holiday. Does he love the snow as much as Carl, or are ten-year-olds too grown up for playing outside now?

I slow as I drive past the Apple store on Main Street. Their display for the latest tech sits in the window, covered in holiday deals. Red and green balloons float above it to draw the eye.

The ad reminds me I haven't been able to text or talk with Angel since their visit last week. They've been without a phone for the better part of the past month because Meg lost hers somehow and needed a replacement Angel couldn't afford to buy.

That makes me wonder if Angel can afford the jump in heating costs the colder weather is bringing. Is there going to be much under the tree for Owen to anticipate? Or Meg? Not for the first time, I consider how easy it would be for me to just go buy them each the latest iPhone.

I can imagine Meg's smile—the mirror image of Angel's gorgeous grin—upon opening up that box. I'd have to get something for Owen to keep things fair. He'd flip for the latest gaming console if he's anything like I was at that age. And maybe whatever fighting game is popular these days. He likes his martial arts classes, so that seems like a solid bet.

Not that I've spent much time with the kids. I've made it a point not to know Angel's children well. No collateral damage when this thing between us inevitably ends. No offering Angel more than friendship with a side of orgasms. But friends buy gifts for their friend's kids, don't they?

I've been getting gifts for Carl's niece for years. She still calls me her uncle, even though we've been divorced longer than she's been alive. Admittedly, not expensive electronics, though.

I resist the temptation to call Angel and ask for their permission. Except I know how that call will go, if Meg even answers, because I keep forgetting that they gave their phone to their kid. Said kid sent me a puking emoji when I texted to ask Angel if they were up the other night. Thank fuck I sent that mostly innocuous question instead of jumping right into text sex. Except I never jump right in with Angel since they prefer a heads up in case the kids are around.

Even if I could get in touch, Angel would only be upset at me for acknowledging the difference in our financial positions. They'd be doing better if their ex paid his child support. But it would definitely cross every line in the book—both professional and personal—to go after the asshole for that. It's still a tempting thought.

Angel won't accept a brand new set of phones. So I need to get creative. I bet if I happen to have a useless spare after I upgrade devices, they won't be too proud to refuse me gifting it to their kid. Especially if I'm underhanded enough to mention the offer via a text Meg will have to pass on to her pop.

Never mind that my current device is barely six months old and perfectly adequate for my needs. I only wish I'd splurged on something fancier back then. They're going to be mad, but I don't care enough to sway me. I want to be able to text Angel without it going through their teenager again. And I want Meg to get the gift she wants without breaking Angel's budget.

I'm pulling into a free spot in front of the store before I've consciously made the decision. I message Carl that I'll meet him at home in a few minutes. It doesn't take long for the helpful customer service agent to set up my new phone with my old number. She resets the old one to its factory default—ready for Meg's SIM card—for a small extra fee. I even get a festive bag to put my old phone in for presenting it to Angel.

I'm whistling and rather pleased with myself as I leave the store, imagining the joy on Meg's face and Angel's reluctant relief upon receiving it. This is not the sort of gesture Carl would have appreciated when we were together, but I enjoy taking care of people in tangible ways like this. There's nothing really romantic about it. Just a practical need met because I can be there for someone I care about.

I text Angel that I got an upgrade, so I have a spare phone for them to give to their kid tomorrow.

Meg texts me back.

Angel: LOL Still Meg. You keep forgetting I have Pop's phone.

Saint: Oops. Sorry about that. Tell your Pop for me?

Angel: Not ur msgr :P but fine w/e

I take a second to decipher that means whatever, though the eye roll emoji that follows it clarifies Meg's opinion of me texting her. Teenagers.

Angel: Thx

I glance at my old phone and smile at the thought of Meg texting all her friends. She can tell them all about how her pop's boring old-dude friend is a massive chump for giving her a phone. I'm okay with that.

Better to be a benevolent annoyance than yet another adult who lets her down.

I park beside Carl in our shared driveway and knock on his door. He greets me with a tumbler full of some sort of gingerbread spiced protein shake that he concocted. He knows how much I love ginger baked goods around the holidays. I always tease him about how he's still my favorite ginger, with his auburn hair. He seems stressed.

"There you are! What took you so long? I have to leave soon." Carl glances at the gift bag I brought inside with me.

"Had a sudden need to upgrade my phone. When is your date?" I glance at the time as I sip my drink. Mm. He's a whiz with a blender. There's the barest hint of lemon under the warm earthy spices that hides the chalky flavor of the protein powder.

"I've got an hour to get ready and drive to the restaurant."

"Okay, relax, babe. You've got plenty of time. Let's see what we're working with." I gesture for him to go up the stairs and he leads the way to his bedroom. I sip more of the drink as we go.

"So, I was thinking chinos and maybe a sweater?" Carl paws through his closet, fingers lingering longingly on some of his more vibrant sweaters.

"Pants first," I suggest. "And put a nice dress shirt under the sweater to class it up a notch."

"Yeah?" He bites his lip as he glances over his shoulder at me.

"Definitely." I nod encouragingly when he pulls out a pair of khaki slacks. Neither of us bats an eye at him changing into them in front of me. The man has a gorgeous ass, which I admire from a purely aesthetic and totally platonic perspective. That ass is off limits. He's asexual and only rarely has any interest in that kind of intimacy. Which is a huge part of why we never could have worked as a couple long-term, in addition to me not meeting his needs.

He rolls his eyes when he notices me ogling him. "My eyes are up here, sailor."

"Uh, huh. They're pretty too, very soulful. I was just checking the pants. Very nice. They really show off your assets." I slurp the last of my drink and set the empty tumbler and my gift bag for Meg on his dresser to deal with later.

Carl rolls his eyes again. "I don't want him to like my *assets*. I want him to like *me*."

"Well, you don't need my help with that part, babe. Just being your lovely, sweet self should seal that deal. But I can make sure you look hot." I reach past him for a purple plaid button up and one of his more muted sweaters, a soft brown boatneck, to show off the shirt.

Carl gives me a dubious look. "Are you sure?"

"Trust me darling, the pop of color will bring out your gorgeous eyes." I pat his furry cheek, then hold the shirt up for him. Carl shrugs into it, letting me fuss over the buttons while he fidgets anxiously. "He's going to love you, and if he doesn't, then it's his loss and you deserve better."

"Agh. You always say that," Carl moans.

"And it's always true. Put on the sweater." I hand it to him. Carl pulls it on obediently. Then he holds out his arms for me to roll up the sleeves of his dress shirt so they lay just so. "Hair." I nudge him toward the washroom. I run some gel through his unruly hair, leaving the rest to him as he brushes his teeth and makes sure his beard is tidy.

"Good?" He poses in front of the mirror, trying to suck in a gut that's utterly perfect for cuddling. He plucks at his pants. "It's not too much?"

"Stop that; you look edible."

"I don't want to be edible." He pouts.

"Well, you always look delicious to me," I tease him with a wink. "So I guess I'm no help to you."

"Saint!" Carl whines my name. He's so damn eager to make a good impression. I get it. I just want him to be with someone who can see how incredible he is. So if this guy is put off by Carl's burly bear good looks and his love of bright colors and soft textures, then it's his loss. Anyone would be lucky to date Carl.

"You seriously look hot, Carl. If he doesn't love you, it's on him."

"Thanks. Okay. I should go, right?"

"Yeah, probably." I nod, following him out of his washroom and toward the stairs, stopping to collect my stuff from his dresser.

"Can I text later to talk about how it goes?" Carl asks. As if he needs permission.

"Any time, babe." I wink at him. "Good luck with the date."

"Thanks. Ah! I'm excited. Fingers crossed, we'll make some Christmas magic." He actually holds up crossed fingers. Freaking adorable man. It's a mystery why he's still single when I know he'd rather be in a relationship. I make a quick detour to deposit my dirty tumbler in his sink.

For Carl's sake, I hope this guy is the one. He deserves to have his perfect holiday romance. Even if it means I get to see him less often. He puts on his shoes and a nice jacket with an earth-toned plaid scarf that's neutral enough to complete his look.

"Mind locking up for me?" Carl asks as we step outside.

"Not at all. Have fun tonight. And let me know how it goes."

"Obviously. Don't wait up." Carl winks at me.

I force a smile and wave to him as he pulls out of our driveway to go meet his date. As I lock his front door before letting myself into my side of the duplex feeling morose. I set the new phone for Meg in the entryway and wish it was tomorrow already, so I'd have company tonight while Carl is hopefully getting swept off his feet. Too bad I can't give Meg the phone tonight, so I could at least talk to Angel. Tomorrow will just have to be soon enough.

Chapter 7

ANGEL (DECEMBER 14TH, 2023)

SAINT GREETS ME AT the door as I'm prying off the fierce calf-hugging faux leather boots I thrifted for Meg last year. She didn't like them, but they're my new favorites. The shearling lining is warmer than most of my other stuff, and I can just cram my feet into them despite their being a size too small.

I've been looking forward to my time with Saint all week. I've been studying my ass off for final exams. That and trying not to have a panic attack every time the kids look longingly at holiday displays for the latest tech they know I can't afford to give them. Meg was practically giddy this morning when she asked if I was going out with Saint tonight. When I pressed, she told me he texted to ask about giving her his old phone.

Sure enough, I look up from ditching my outerwear to see my stress relief dangling a gift bag from the Apple store in front of me. I'm going to kill Saint, and the bemused yet apologetic expression on his face tells me he knows exactly how I feel about him manipulating me into taking expensive gifts.

"You really fucking suck sometimes, Mathieu." I first-name him, because I don't appreciate him popping the illusion that I can have this time to lay down my burdens. Just a few hours where I can be an adult who gets to enjoy myself with another adult.

He keeps holding up the bag, a flicker of concern crossing his eyes as he wiggles it enticingly. I reluctantly snatch it from him. There's no good way to tell him no, but accepting expensive gifts from a lover makes my stomach roil.

"I do. I thought you liked that about me?" he teases with a lazy jerking off motion when I turn back to face him, arms crossed protectively over my chest.

"You can't buy me a new phone every time Trev—Meg loses hers." Fuck. I expressly did not tell him that Meg's father is the reason she no longer has her old phone. Trevor told her he didn't want her texting in her bedroom. When he caught her doing it anyway, he confiscated the phone. He claims disobeying him is proof Meg is too immature to have her own phone.

Nevermind my pleas to return it to her when she is at my place so she can call for rides or in an emergency. Not to mention the fact I pay for it and her phone plan.

It's ridiculous, because I can kind of understand his reasoning for the rule. I wasn't that much older than Meg is now when I started dating him. That's nothing I want to think about. Meg is far savvier than I was. And more interested in dance than boys. Or girls.

Saint sobers immediately. Damnation—it's entirely unfair how hot he is when he hones that laser-sharp lawyerly authority on me.

"What exactly happened to Meg's old phone?" Saint stalks a step closer, hand planted on his hip in a pose that emphasizes his gym honed muscles.

"I told you; she lost it." I can't meet his gaze and lie, so I stare at those bulging biceps.

"How?"

I set my jaw. "I plead the fifth."

"The US constitution doesn't apply in Ontario, Angel." Saint caresses my cheek, but his tone softens. "And I very much doubt the answer to that question would be self-incrimination."

We're at an impasse and my time is ticking. Saint might have other hookups, but this is all the me-time I can afford to allot myself beyond the occasional extra long shower if I get up early enough. Less than two hours a week that are all mine to indulge with this man. I'm not wasting them over something stupid. I sigh.

"Trevor took it and refuses to return it."

"For the love of..." Saint makes an outraged sound of frustration and I watch the conflicting emotions play across his face. I know he's not angry at me, but it still makes me uncomfortable to see him mad. "Let me get this straight. You bought the phone for her?"

"Yeah. Still paying it off."

Saint's jaw ticks. "And you requested it back?"

"Of course."

"And he refused? So he kept possession of your property while continuing to renege on his court-ordered financial obligations?"

"That pretty much sums it up." I shrug. I just want this conversation to be over. So we can get to the part where he rails me until I don't have room for anything in my brain but how good he makes me feel.

"Angel. For the love of fuck, let me at least file a motion to get your kids their money from him."

Goddamn fucking lawyer, knowing just how to word things to twist the knife and make me consider accepting his charity.

"That's playing dirty, Saint."

"I know. And I'm sorry, but you are working yourself to the bone and I want to help you. Let me help?"

"I can't. It will be fine. I'm almost done with school, and then things will get better. Just have to pass my finals, and then I can start my practicum."

"Student teaching? As in adding working ridiculous hours for even more ridiculous pay on top of everything else you're already doing? Angel, that's—" He shakes his head, thinking better of whatever insult was on the tip of his tongue at my glare "—Let me help you. I can go after back child support for you."

"No. It's not worth going after Trevor, and I can't afford to pay you."

Saint shakes his head at me. "You want my legal opinion on that?"

"No. I've used you more than enough for today." I shake my head and brandish the bag with the new phone that will make Meg's Christmas. The man plays dirtier than an entire week's worth of the cloth diaper laundry I used to do for the kids when they were babies. I don't give him any more ammunition by pointing out that I actually have to pay for the privilege of doing my student teaching.

"You can use me any way you like, Angel." Saint steps closer, tentatively reaching toward my face. I lean into his gentle caress, the sweet touches I've been craving since I left his place a week ago.

"Fuck you." I hiss the words, eyes closed, unwilling to deny myself, but angry at him for how he went about this. Furious at myself for being angry and for making him believe the only way I'd accept his help is if he went behind my back. Not to mention using my kid to manipulate me. That's fucked up, and I'm not sure which of us is the bigger asshole for it.

"Is that what you want? Because I am game for it." He tries to turn it into a joke and I'm not in the mood to laugh. Everything is just so overwhelming. I came here tonight to set all of it down, if only for a few hours. It sucks that he's throwing my failures in my face. Not on purpose...but still.

"You know what? Forget it. Thanks for the phone. I should go." I turn to put my boots back on, but I can't quite manage the coordination with my eyes blurry from suppressed tears. My heart is pounding with all these conflicting feelings. Sick to my stomach at the prospect of choosing between more credit card debt or explaining to Owen why his sister got another new phone while he gets socks.

Fuck my life. I guess I could give Owen my phone once I give Meg this one. I'd planned on waiting another few years before handing Owen that kind of responsibility, but...

Saint touches my shoulder.

"Did I fuck this up?" he asks when I glance back at him.

"Yeah." I swipe my hand over my eyes to dash away the tears. "I'm exhausted, Saint. There aren't enough hours in the day and I can't pay you back for this or afford to get Owen something with a similar value and I just..."

He purses his lips. "If I offer to buy your son an Xbox to make it even, would that make things worse?"

I laugh then, but it sounds bitter, because of course that's nothing to him. He can just throw more money at me and I'll smile and thank him and...I don't know what his endgame is.

Most likely, knowing Saint, he just wants to make my life easier. But the thought of strings tied to his gifts makes me want to run before I can find out otherwise. There was a time when I didn't think Trevor's affection came with obligations and I was so catastrophically wrong. I won't go back to living like that.

"Right, I'll take that as a yes." Saint rubs at his neck.

He looks so earnest, like he's upset to watch me having a breakdown in his entryway. This didn't have to happen. We could have just gone up to his room. We could be basking in the afterglow by now.

"I don't want you to solve my problems for me, Saint. I don't want to be dependent on anyone." Not ever again.

"I'm sorry. If it's that big a deal, I can take the phone back."

I bark out a laugh. "Except you went behind my back and told Meg about it already. Which, honestly, might be the worst part. You can't use my kids to manipulate me like that again, Mathieu. Or we're through, got me?"

"You're right. That was a shitty judgment call. But you needed a phone, and I knew you wouldn't take the gift for yourself."

"You're right. Saint, this isn't normal. Fuck buddies, don't just gift each other brand new iPhones."

"I know. That's why it's my old one." He smiles at me, inviting me in on the joke, but it's too much.

"Didn't you just get a new phone over the summer?"

"Yes?" He winces theatrically, and I know he's still trying to cheer me up.

I burst out laughing then, I can't help it, I laugh until I'm doubled over and my sides ache and Saint reaches to steady me, patting my back.

"I'm glad you find me so hilarious." He pouts at me.

"You twisted yourself into a pretzel to justify this, huh?"

"A tiny bit?" He tugs at his salt-and-pepper hair. "Ugh. Look, you're my friend above anything else that's between us."

"Okay?"

"So, the thing is, when I tell people I don't do relationships, they usually get the wrong idea. Like, they assume it means I'm some sort of emotionless robot. Or they decide they can change me with the power of true love." He rolls his eyes.

I snort. "The power of love is a steaming pile of unicorn shit."

"See? This is why we work so well." Saint grins sheepishly at me. "The thing is, just because I'm not going to suddenly profess my undying love for you in skywriting doesn't mean I don't care about you, Angel."

"Yeah, I know you do." I force a smile. "I'm still mad at you, but I get why you did it and I'll get over it."

"Do you get it? Because friendships are important to me. I enjoy helping my friends. Do you know how much it kills me to watch you struggling when I could help you without a second thought?"

I swallow hard. It's been obvious he cares about me for ages. I'm just squirmy at the acknowledgement. I don't want what we have to change. More upheaval is the last thing I need in my life.

"Do *you* know how much it sucks knowing you could wave your bank account around and solve all the problems that keep me up at night? But I've been there before, Saint. Stuck resenting someone who made me miserable because he could give me a more comfortable life. I would rather struggle on my own forever than be reliant on someone again. Even you."

"That's..." Saint sucks in a long breath. "I don't like that. Sometimes the things you say make me wish I'd convinced you to go scorched earth in the divorce settlement, Angel. I would take your ex back to court for the sheer pleasure of getting a judge to garnish his wages. I'd love nothing more than to see him held accountable for a fraction of what he's put you and your kids through."

"He's not that bad." I don't know why I defend Trevor, except he's still someone my kids love.

"If you say so." Saint shakes his head, but he doesn't contradict me. He opens his arms to me. "I'm sorry I upset you. Will you forgive me?"

"You're forgiven." I sigh as I let myself fall into his arms. It might be impossible to let myself take everything he's willing to offer me, but I can take this comfort. His arms around me, patting my back and making me feel cared for in ways no one has in so, so long. I lean against him, enjoying his strength.

"I don't suppose you'd consider letting me make it up to you by getting Owen something to even the scales?" Saint's eyes twinkle as he pushes his luck. I trace his lips with my fingers. If I had it in me to give my heart away again, I could fall for his sweet smile.

"You just can't help yourself, can you?" I snuggle into his embrace.

"Not at all. But I seriously do feel bad for using your kid against you like that. Let me do penance?" Saint's hands at the small of my back press me closer, a reassuring comfort.

I roll my eyes and let myself have the breathing room Saint is offering. "He wants the latest Xbox. Don't go too wild on the games."

"Done and done." Saint kisses my neck and I arch to give him better access, even as my bits throb with arousal.

"Take me to bed?" I ask, because I don't have much time left to spend with him tonight, and I want every part of him that I can allow myself.

"That would be my absolute pleasure." Saint takes my hand, gallantly kissing it before he leads me up the stairs. He's gentler than usual, and I cling to him tighter when he's thrusting into me. I don't let myself think of it as making love. It's just sex.

Phenomenal sex, his dick stretching me open with every pump of his hips, his fingers slick as he rubs Bitsy in time to his strokes. Saint kisses me until the friction and warmth of his body moving with mine transports me. To a reality where I can have this. Pleasure and someone who wants to share it with me.

Neither of us wants it to end, and for a blissful window of time, it doesn't have to. We move together and keep up the gentle climb toward orgasm. But eventually it's too good, too much. I'm too close to hold back any longer. The need to come is an aching thing deep inside my belly. My thighs tremble with the effort of holding myself back.

I kiss along Saint's throat, to his shoulder, where I muffle the sound of his name against his skin when I come. He isn't far behind me in finishing, as if he was waiting until I reached my climax. His cock pulses inside me and I move with him, wanting to draw out these last moments of connection for as long as possible.

Moments like this, I wish we had more time. More nights where I don't have to clean up and rush out the door. More of Saint's steady presence making it seem like everything will turn out just fine and giving me reasons to smile.

Chapter 8

ANGEL (DECEMBER 16TH, 2023)

LUCK WAS ON MY side the past few weeks. I aced my finals and I might pull off a perfect Christmas for my kids. Between Saint's generosity and my boss letting me pick up several lucrative evening and weekend shifts, there is going to be plenty under the tree this year. I only had to stoop to asking Meg to watch her brother for one of those shifts; that's always my last resort.

Owen and Meg have been going to holiday parties at their friends' houses and spending time with their uncle while I work in the lead up to the holidays. My brother and his wife offered to take my kids holiday shopping with them tonight, and they agreed to keep them overnight so I can work.

About halfway through my shift, my luck runs out. Trevor is sitting in my section. I almost turn right back around and duck into the kitchen to hide until he leaves. Trevor catches my eye and jumps up to wave me down. I sigh and go to face my fate.

"Hey, can we talk?" Trevor asks. He must want something. He's usually more the type for demanding, but he actually seems nervous, fiddling with his napkin.

I glance meaningfully at the busy restaurant, hoping he'll read the room, but of course it would never occur to him that ambushing me at work is a shitty move. Or that I'm too busy to deal with him.

"What do you need?"

"Nothing. Well, except you know how I said you could keep the kids for my next weekend?"

"Yeah?" My stomach clenches. Christmas. He's going to take Christmas away from me. No. But there's not a hell of a lot I can do about it. I can say no, but it *is* his weekend and I don't want to stick the kids in the middle of a fight.

"I'm going to need them to come over after all."

"Why?"

"I got a new job."

"Okay?" I'm not sure how that's relevant, but I'm sure Trevor will enlighten me.

"It's in Alberta. So, I won't be around. I want to take the kids to my mom's in Hamilton for the holidays, sort of a goodbye visit before I move out there."

Oh shit. My stomach sinks down to my toes. This sounds like a tectonic shift in our co-parenting. "When do you leave?"

I just want to stomp my feet and throw a gigantic tantrum at the unfairness of it all, but I need this job—at least for a little while longer. There goes my happy holiday with my kids. Not to mention what a move will mean for their relationship with Trevor. I'm on autopilot as I gather the information I need from him, trying to numb out the loss so I can make it through the rest of my shift before I break down.

"I'm flying out on New Year's Day," Trevor says. As though it's totally normal to uproot your kids' lives on a week's notice. Fuck. I can't stand the infuriating man right now. Most of the time, if I'm honest.

"How is that going to impact our visitation schedule? Do you want them to visit in the summer, or—"

Trevor shakes his head, like I'm being obtuse. "You don't get it. This is goodbye, Angie. I've seen your shitbox car at that lawyer's place. I'm not coming back to let you come after me for more of my money. Half the town knows you've been sleeping with him to pay off your legal fees."

I ignore the dig about my sex life, even if the idea that Saint did something shady by sleeping with me makes my skin crawl. Saint doesn't deserve to be thrown into the rumor mill, but people like to talk. It's just human nature. I don't care about my name being linked with his. Hopefully, Saint isn't upset about any rumors linking the two of us either.

I want to scoff at Trevor, ask him *what money?* He hasn't paid me a single loonie of child support in over a year. But I just shake my head.

"Anyway. I'm making a clean break of it. Starting with a fresh slate out west. So, here's the deal: you give me Christmas with my mom and don't get any funny ideas about taking me back to court. In return, I won't sue for sole custody and take the brats with me."

It's an empty threat. There's no way he could actually do that. Fear still curdles in the pit of my stomach and claws at my throat. I can't breathe past the horror of his threat.

"Okay," I croak. "You can have Christmas."

Trevor smiles, but it's the cruel smile he gets when he knows he's won. There's not an ounce of warmth in his expression, and his eyes are cold as he looks down his nose at me.

I press my order pad against my chest, wishing I could be anywhere but here. "I'll pick them up Monday afternoon. When do you expect to get back from visiting your mom?"

"You can pick them up from my place after presents, say around five? She wants to eat early, so that should be plenty of time to drive back."

"Okay. I'll be there." And I'll text to make him confirm our plan in writing later. The exchange leaves me numb as I take his order. Because, of course he has the audacity to stick around and make me give him service with a smile after dropping his bombshell on me. I take some small solace in knowing that my lack of a visible response irks him. But mostly I'm reeling.

Owen is going to be devastated when he realizes Trevor isn't coming back. Meg might be relieved not to be forced into semi-regular visits at first. But it's still going to hurt to hear Trevor is planning on walking out of their lives without a backward glance. I'm not sure what to do about the news.

Do I tell the kids? Give them a heads-up that the family memories he suddenly wants to give them on Christmas are meant as a goodbye? Or do I let him share the news in his own time? Sideswipe them with it at the last minute? Or just watch the hope slowly die in Owen's eyes when Trevor strings him along with promised visits that never materialize? I can't handle that. And then there's the legal side of it all.

By the time my shift ends, I'm itching to call Saint. I need advice. Not legal advice, per se. Just a listening ear who isn't so close to this emotionally. I need a friend. And I need it before I see my kids and blurt out words I'll regret. Hell, I need to figure out which words those would be.

Fuck. Now I'm going to have to break it to Meg that our cozy Christmas at home isn't happening. Owen will be excited to see his cousins at least. Saint's contact practically begs me to hit the call button. We almost never call. Texting, sure. All the time. Stupid shit. I sent him a picture of some eclairs we got in yesterday. One exploded during delivery, so it looked like it had gotten a little too—er, *excited*—to be eaten.

Last night, he texted me that Carl roped him into a movie night and they were watching *Elf*, so we spent a solid hour exchanging GIFs from the movie. I tried to convince the kids to watch the same movie with me again, but they weren't into it. Owen and I ended up playing with his LEGOs while Meg texted her friends.

I bite my lip as I hover my finger over the call button. It would be so amazing to hear his voice. I send Saint the GIF with Will Ferrell hugging the raccoon and a caption that reads, 'Someone needs a hug.' It's me.

I don't expect an immediate reply, so I'm still debating whether a call is too much when he replies.

Saint: Rough shift tonight?

Angel: You could say that.

Saint: Are you the someone who needs a hug?

I'm tempted to play it off like a joke. It's too much to ask, right? I don't want to push him away by demanding too much from him. He isn't my boyfriend and coming to him all needy and begging for emotional support is only going to make him think that's what I want from him. It's not, he's just become one of my closest friends, somehow. If I can't go to him for comfort, then who?

Marcus? My brother's tree farm is in the midst of the busy season and he's expecting his first kid. I'm lucky he and his wife have been as helpful as they've been lately. Carl is always friendly with me, but we aren't friends. Even if it seems like I know him from how much Saint talks about him.

Saint: Want to talk about it? Or can you come over?

Angel: Is that an invitation?

Saint: Yeah. If the kids are alright without you for a while longer?

Angel: Marcus said I can pick them up in the morning since I ended up with a closing shift today.

Saint: Come on over then. Should I crack open the wine? Or I can warm up some of that cider you liked the other night.

Angel: Hot cider sounds good.

Angel: Thanks.

Saint: See you soon?

Angel: Yeah.

I just have to finish cleaning the floor in my section before I ditch. I check to be sure that Marcus and Gail haven't texted about any change in plans or that the kids need me. But all's quiet on that front and soon I'm pulling up in front of Saint's place.

I text that I'm there, and he opens the door as I'm walking up the front steps.

"Hey there, Angel." He opens his arms to me and I hug him in his entryway.

"Hey," I mumble into his shoulder.

While his arms wrap around me, my burdens seem lighter. As if I don't have to carry them alone. Even if that's an illusion, it's comforting. I cling to him until Saint shuffles his feet, antsy at the prolonged hugging.

"Kitchen or bedroom?" Saint asks, tempting me to just keep my mouth shut and let him drown out my worries with pleasure instead of dealing with the hard things. Well. The *difficult* things. I'm plenty interested in his hard cock digging into my hip before I step back to deal with my snowy boots.

"Kitchen." I gesture.

"What's up?" Saint asks, leading the way to the steaming mugs he's already set out with a plate of festive cookies. He catches me looking at the gingerbread and smiles. "Carl brought those over last night. He had a few extra."

"Ah, so you're foisting leftovers off on me?" I joke, putting off the conversation I came here to have. I'm not sure where to start. Talking about Trevor is always a mood killer.

Saint shrugs, then he grabs a cookie and bites off its cute little head. "They're pretty good."

"I'm sure they are." I sit and take a cookie. But I don't have the appetite to eat it now that I'm thinking about what brought me here in the first place. I break off an arm and crumble it into smaller pieces between my fingers. "Gingerbread?"

"Yep. I'm a sucker for all those warm holiday spices."

"Mm. If you're a ginger fan, did Marcus ever bring you Gran's gingerbread swirl fudge?" I smile just thinking of the sweet confection.

It's been ages since I tasted Gran's fudge. I never got the family recipe. I should see if Marcus has it. Or get him to ask Mom for it if not. He's been making so much more of an effort. His vying for uncle of the year lately still doesn't feel like enough to make up for past hurts, but I could try meeting his attempts at reconciliation halfway. Especially if it means getting that little taste of Gran's love back.

"I haven't. That sounds delicious. Nothing beats homemade fudge. But you can't distract me with sweets, Angel. Tell me what happened?"

"Trever came in tonight." I drop my gaze to the table, watching as if the crumbs I'm nudging around my plate are fascinating, so I don't have to see him get upset.

"Did he—" Saint's hackles go up immediately.

I rush to reassure him. Perfect. This is why I should keep shit to myself. How am I the one defending Trevor's crappy behavior yet again?

"No, he paid his bill and everything." I make myself meet Saint's concerned gaze. "You know how I told you he agreed to swap weekends with me so I could have the kids home for Christmas and then he'd get New Year's?"

"Yeah?"

"He changed his mind. Now he wants them for the holiday."

"But you usually have them back on Sunday evening, so you'd still get them for Christmas Eve night, right?"

I shake my head. "He asked to keep them until after the holiday meal at his mom's on Monday. And he told me he has to switch back because he's moving to Alberta after the holidays. He threatened to go after custody if I make a fuss."

Saint stills my cookie-crumbling fingers by placing his warm palm over my hand and pressing it to the table until I look at him. "Angel, there is no way in hell a court is going to give him custody."

"How can you be sure?"

"Are you kidding me?" The look Saint gives me makes me feel small and clueless. His entire demeanor softens, his eyes locked onto mine. "Angel, I know you're scared because that sniveling amoeba knows how to hit you where it hurts. But—and you know how hesitant I am to make any promises about litigation—I swear to you, that will not happen."

I stare at Saint, because he's told me in the past that he can't make that kind of sweeping promise. Honestly, though, in this case, he's probably right. I don't even think Trevor would actually try it. He wants to hurt me, but he's never had the patience for the actual work of parenting. Trevor wouldn't burden himself with that kind of responsibility just to punish me for the perceived slight of choosing Saint over him. Or whatever he's twisted the situation into in his head.

Besides, Saint is just a friend. A really good friend. Probably the best friend I could imagine, honestly.

"Yeah?" I choke out, past the fear clogging my throat.

"Yeah." Saint sounds so confident, and I'm desperate to trust in his promises. He ticks off his points on his fingers. "Trevor hasn't paid his child support in ages. He makes a habit of missing visitation, which you have documented extensively. He's planning to move across the country to a different province, which would complicate visitation. And if this is the first you are hearing about a move that's less than a month away, then he's already in violation of the Divorce Act. He needed to give you at least sixty days of formal notice for a relocation. Plus, the kids are established here. They have family ties, school, activities, and you've always been their primary caretaker."

I bite my lip, still shaky with nerves and not quite ready to dismiss the worst-case scenario.

"*And* if he actually tries it, I will absolutely be representing you. Pro bono, because I won't sit by and watch that asshole try to take your kids away while there is still breath in my body. You got me?"

"Yeah." I take a shuddery breath and try to let myself believe Saint. "I told him yes to Christmas."

"Are you okay with that?" Saint's piercing gaze tells me he already knows the answer.

I'm not. Not really. I'm going to miss the heck out of my kids. It will be awful, sitting in my empty apartment staring at the presents Saint helped me put under the tree, despite my reservations.

"I want them to have one last memory before he goes, something to make them feel loved when he's gone. He said he doesn't want to bother with visitation once he moves. How the fuck do I tell my babies that he doesn't want them anymore?"

That's the thing that's going to break me. I am intimately familiar with what it's like to be thrown out like that. Trevor has my blessing to fuck with me as much as he wants, whenever he wants, if it would spare them that hurt. I stayed with him for years to spare them that hurt. Until I figured out that nothing I did was ever going to change my ex or his hot, then cold indifference to the kids.

Saint comes around the table to hold me while I crumble under the weight of the pain I can't spare Meg and Owen.

"Hey, it's going to be okay, Angel. They'll be okay. You'll make sure of it."

His lips brush my temple as he murmurs meaningless platitudes. And I let him comfort me. He's the only one I let in like this. My safe space. The one who gets to see me broken open and scooped hollow. When I finally get myself back under control, he reheats my cider for me and we sit there in companionable silence, sipping our drinks.

"Come over on Christmas?" Saint offers.

"You sure?" I didn't expect that from him. We spend a lot of my kid-free nights together lately, but that's about sex. An invite to spend a holiday together seems big. Like we're something to each other. More than casual friends who sometimes fuck. Well, duh. I suppose buying my kids pricey electronics isn't particularly casual either. Except to him, it sort of is?

Saint hesitates, then he nods. "Yeah. You shouldn't have to be alone. Carl and I usually make cinnamon buns or something and eat ourselves into a sugar coma on Christmas morning."

"Mm. Sounds delicious." I can't help a twinge of disappointment that Carl is part of the plan. Like Saint needs to remind me that this is a friendly gesture, nothing more, and I shouldn't read anything into the invitation. I wouldn't, but he seems so convinced I will whenever I lean on him for support. It's a bit infuriating that he thinks I'm—what? Hiding some massive crush? I'm over the concept of romance, and my stance on that won't change just from him being a good friend to me.

"We can make extra for you to bring to the kiddos."

Though, if he was trying to score boyfriend points, he couldn't do better than offering kindness to my kids.

"They would like that."

I'm no closer to having answers about what to do, but Saint makes me feel like I don't have to face it alone. I'll have to take the Trevor situation as it comes. It might be time to look at going back to that family counselor we went to during the divorce proceedings. She might have answers on the best course forward for the kids. If I can get an appointment, I'll figure out how to cover the costs later.

"Ready for bed?" Saint asks as I nibble at the remains of my destroyed cookie.

"I'm not really in the mood." I hunch my shoulders, hoping he doesn't push. So far there haven't been strings on his friendship. But I showed up out of the blue and snotted all over him tonight, so if he expects...

"To sleep, Angel. I can read a room." Saint nudges me and I flush in embarrassed relief. Saint isn't an asshole. Someday I might get that memo and stop assuming everyone is like Trevor.

"Yeah. You sure you don't mind me staying over?"

"Not in the least. Come on." He offers me his hand and hauls me to my feet when I take it.

He lends me an oversized t-shirt to sleep in and the spare toothbrush I've been using for months when I have a weekend night with him. Saint isn't my boyfriend. But he's the best friend I could ask for right now.

No part of me wanted to go home to my empty apartment tonight. I keep the heat on practically arctic when the kids aren't around. So instead of shivering alone in my lumpy twin bed and staring at my water-stained ceiling for hours, tossing and turning over what Trevor's news will mean for me and the kids, I drop off to sleep with Saint's warm body tucked up against my back. His big hand is splayed over my belly, pinning me close to him, filling my senses with him and the pavlovian sense that I'm safe here in his bed.

Chapter 9

SAINT (DECEMBER 21ST, 2023)

ANGEL SHOWING UP AT my door is usually the highlight of my week. So I try to dismiss the nerves that go through me at the crinkled gift bag they have with them when they show up late the Thursday before Christmas. They can't afford fancy gifts, and we both know it. And exchanging presents seems too much like the trappings of a relationship.

"Everything alright?" I ask, ignoring the gift while they deal with their snowy, calf-hugging boots.

"Yeah." Angel sighs, scraping their long beautiful hair back out of their face. I've made a study of that sweet face, cheekbones that have become more pronounced over the weeks and months as their jawline gets wider and more masculine. The patchy stubble that infuriates them with how slowly it's been filling in. They can't quite hide the perennial exhaustion around their stormy ocean blue eyes. Angel has always been attractive, but their smile is stunning, even when it's strained and wobbly around the edges. "Well, no, but I'll figure it out. The freaking car wouldn't start."

"Shit." It's on the tip of my tongue to offer whatever help they need. But my eyes stick on the ominous gift bag. Fair or not, it screams relationship, so I keep the offer to myself.

"Yeah. Marcus said he'd look at it in the morning. I've got my fingers crossed it's the battery and all I need is a quick jump. But the boss said it was fine to leave it in the lot at work overnight, so it could be worse."

They shrug it off like a minor inconvenience when I know it could represent an expense big enough to break the camel's back for them.

"Fingers crossed." I do just that, holding up both hands for them to see, gratified when they smile at the corny gesture.

"Anyway, I made you something." They shove the bag toward me.

"Oh, you shouldn't have." I swallow hard.

My gut impulse to reject the offering is hypocritical as fuck after I wheedled them into accepting gifts for their kids. But that feels different. Helping my friend give their kids an amazing holiday isn't the same as a thoughtful, homemade gift between lovers. I take the bag and peek reluctantly past the snow-soggy tissue paper that looks the worse for Angel's trek over here.

Angel rolls their eyes. "It's nothing fancy. I just got Gran's recipe from Marcus and you mentioned you like gingerbread, so I thought—is it okay?"

I open the bag to find the adorable tin of homemade fudge. The other night, I offhandedly mentioned wanting to try their family recipe, and here it is. This should make me happy, but it reminds me too viscerally of the sort of heartfelt gift Carl would have gotten me when we were romantically involved. I can't parse all the emotions roiling through me.

Deeply thoughtful and personal, Angel's gift scares me. Angel is going through a lot with their ex, their kids, finishing their teaching program in the spring, and now their car crapping out on them. I can't be the boyfriend who stands by their side and supports them through all that. Friend, yes. Boyfriend? The mere thought gives me hives.

There's too much baggage there. Angel knows I'm aromantic and what that means for me when it comes to dating. It's too much for me to process what it will mean for us if they see me as something other than a friend who they enjoy fucking. I'm taking too long to respond to the sweet gesture.

Angel's face falls. I could kick myself for making it weird when I've been looking forward to seeing them all week. I wish this could be as simple as enjoying each other's company, but it never is.

"Saint?" Angel says my name like a plea and it kills me not to be able to give them the reaction they want. "It's not a love declaration. Just some fudge."

"Looks great. Thanks." I tuck the tin back into the bag and hang it on the hook near my keys. Guilt wracks me as I pretend not to see their hurt expression. I need to move this entire encounter back onto less fraught emotional ground. "So, down to fuck?"

"Yeah." Angel glances between me and the bag. They lick their lips, like they want to say something more about it, or take back the weirdness. Fuck knows that I want to take that back. But they don't say another thing about it.

We go upstairs and I spend a solid hour with my mouth on them, apologizing for everything I can't put into words by making them come. I revel in making them tremble and shake, moaning incoherent encouragement. I can't promise them more than we've got, but I can try to show them how wonderful everything is just the way we are. Remind them what we have works and shouldn't be messed with.

Or I might need to remind myself. I'm the one who pushed to treat each other like friends and not just a recurring hookup. I'm the one who started the gift giving. This is all on me.

I'm an asshole. And I can't seem to stop myself as I roll out of bed before their sweat has cooled and pull on my robe. That isn't how we normally end the night, but I justify it to myself because they'll need extra time to get Owen from tae kwon do without their car. Angel watches me with wide, hurt eyes.

"Guess I should get going?"

"Don't want to leave Owen wondering where you are." I scratch at my stubble and turn away so I'm not tempted to get dressed and offer to give them a ride. Or lend them my car. Distance. We need distance.

"Right. Thanks for tonight, Saint."

"My pleasure, as always."

"Pretty sure tonight was all my pleasure." They dart a reproachful glance toward my crotch. I guess I didn't have them so distracted they didn't notice I didn't come tonight. That hasn't happened with them in ages, but I wasn't really in the mood with worry about losing them gnawing at the edges of my awareness. If they're falling for me, I can't keep this up. So if being a little cool with them forestalls that... it's less cruel than encouraging them.

I can't resist watching them dress in their work clothes from earlier. I'll miss that view when this ends. The lovely curve of their hips, the dimpled perfection of their naked ass. How their hair cascades over their bare shoulders. Angel gives me a tight smile when they catch me watching them. I walk them back downstairs.

We both glance at the gift bag dangling by the door. Then Angel struggles back into their too-small boots. If I was going to get them a gift for the holiday, it would be proper warm boots that actually fit. No matter how good their legs look in their current pair with a slight heel.

I hold the door open for Angel before I can get caught up in how precious they've become to me and break down to offer them a ride.

"Bye, Saint. I don't need the tin back." Angel's gaze lingers on my face, hopeful.

Behind Angel, I catch a glimpse of Carl's new beau, Nick, approaching. My mood sours further. Carl is so excited about their date tonight. Nick better live up to the hype. As long as he keeps making my bestie happy, my personal feelings of loss at potentially being demoted from the most important person in my dearest friend's life don't matter. Not as long as he's what Carl wants. But does everything really have to unravel all at once, right now?

"Yeah. Okay." I sound churlish and distracted, but I need to create distance.

"Call me?" Angel holds their finger and thumb up to the side of their face and I'm struck by the absurdity of that gesture in the age of cellphones. Their kids would probably laugh at it.

Wind gusts and I tug my robe tighter closed. It's cold. Once more, I have to bite my tongue against offering that ride. I don't want them freezing, but there are other ways I can offer help.

"Here." I grab an extra scarf from the hall closet and loop it around Angel's neck. I wish I could drape them in cashmere all the time. Warm them up and keep them safe. But I can't blur the parameters of our friendship anymore than I already have. It's not fair. Not to either of us.

Our eyes lock as I tug them in closer to adjust the scarf around their neck. Angel kisses me, and I don't have the willpower to deny myself one more taste of their lips. I clutch the soft scarf like a lifeline as I kiss Angel goodbye.

Should I reconsider our Christmas plans? It might be time to have another heart-to-heart about what we are to each other. And what I can never be to them.

"Bye, Angel." I release my grip on the scarf and steer them out the door.

"Bye, Saint." They cast one last wistful glance at me over their shoulder before trudging off into the night. Only half paying attention to my conversation with Nick, I can't tear my gaze off Angel huddling against the cold. I admonish Nick to treat my bestie right even as I watch Angel turn out of sight. Yeah, I'm already kicking myself for being a massive hypocrite. This is not treating Angel the way they deserve.

I should have offered to drive them. It's dark and the roads aren't great and they shouldn't have to walk home in the snow with their kid in this weather. If I throw on some clothes now, I can catch Angel before they get to the community center that hosts Owen's tae kwon do classes. I'll worry about the consequences of that offer later.

Chapter 10

ANGEL (DECEMBER 21ST, 2023)

I DON'T KNOW HOW well I hid my disappointment with Saint's reaction to the fudge. He might as well have dumped it in the trash bin with the way he looked at my meager holiday offering. I figured since Carl brought him cookies, holiday treats between friends were acceptable gifts. Apparently I thought wrong. Or he just doesn't want food *from me*.

That stings, but I'll get over it. I've got the entire trek to get Owen and take him home to let those emotions cool down. At least walking is getting my blood pumping and keeping me mostly warm.

The scarf Saint draped around my neck is so cozy and it smells like his cologne, woodsy and comforting. Maybe I should have refused to take it from him after he rejected my gift, but it's freezing. I can always give it back to him during our next visit.

My adrenaline pounds when a car pulls alongside me halfway to the community center. I lengthen my stride and hunch my shoulders. At first, I stare resolutely straight ahead, just keeping the moving vehicle in my periphery.

Really, I doubt that ignoring it will help. Since when does ignoring assholes actually make them go away? It's a toss up whether whoever is rolling down the driver's side window is winding up to hurl slurs or catcalls at me. Or their own unoriginal blending of the two.

"Hey, darling. Need a ride?"

I startle at the familiar voice when it comes. I do a double take. It's really Saint gazing at me from the toasty warm interior of his Mercedes with concern in his eyes.

I bite my cheek. There has to be a reason he didn't offer me a ride from the start. My pride rebels at the idea of accepting the favor when he couldn't even look at me properly over the fudge. But it's cold and I want to be warm. I want to be someone who can depend on another person for a ride home. The prospect of lugging all of Owen's gear home on foot with him tired and complaining about the long walk tips the scales.

"If it's not too much trouble?"

"No trouble at all. I just remembered I'm out of cream for my coffee so I needed to drive this way regardless. Hop in." Saint leans across the console to pop open the passenger side door. I scoot around the front of his vehicle and get in, luxuriating in the heat blasting from the vents.

"Ah, morning catastrophe averted." My joke is tepid.

Saint cracks the tiniest of smiles. His excuse for following me rings hollow, but it lets us both save face. We can go back to pretending things between us aren't off kilter. If I had to pinpoint when things changed for me, it would be the phone he bought for Meg. I shiver violently. My jacket isn't really up for another Ontario winter.

"It's got heated seats." Saint gestures at the dash that's lit up with enough features to rival a Christmas display.

"Thanks." I jab at the buttons to turn it on, darting surreptitious glances at Saint. His car practically glides along the streets to the community center with a smoothness that has nothing to do with the icy conditions. This thing rides so much nicer than my old car. I wish I could spend a lot longer admiring Saint's profile as I wonder how everything got so freaking complicated.

The thing is, I'm not looking for romance. It's just that taking care of my kids has been my sole responsibility for so long, I've forgotten what it's like to be the one cared for. I don't think Saint fully comprehends how much his simple gestures mean to me. How his constant and ongoing kindness is like kryptonite to my heart.

I can see myself falling for him. Getting used to having someone in my corner. Someone who holds me when I can't hold myself together for a second longer. Who offers me help when it seems like the next disaster will shatter me.

And that's terrifying because I promised I'd never put myself in that position again. Never depend on someone else when everyone I've ever loved has done such an excellent job of showing me how fast comfort and support can be ripped away. Our friendship's framework started out so clear. Fuck buddies. Easy, no-strings sex and the occasional raunchy joke over text.

But it evolved from there. Of course it did. I don't think I could stop myself from caring for the man who holds me after a bad day and lets me vent about a shitty shift at work if I tried. And Saint cares too, it's obvious in all our interactions.

I love him. Best friend love. The first person I call when I get important news love. Like Trevor moving. Or the email that pings my inbox as I fumble over the fancy controls for Saint's heated seats. They're nice, but my butt might ignite if I leave it set to the hottest setting for long.

I punch the off button, immediate relief as the burning heat subsides to a gentle glow. The email is even better.

"I got my transitional certification from the province!"

"Huh?" He glances over at me, eyes darting over my body like he thinks I'm talking about something related to my gender transition. I bite my lip so I won't laugh at the unasked questions burning in his interested gaze. He turns back to the road before I can remind him to pay attention and doesn't pry for details.

"It's for teaching. You know how I'm starting my practicum in January?"

"Oh! I was going to say I didn't think you needed a certificate to transition." He forces a chuckle. "But yeah, you've mentioned that."

"Well, I've been in touch with my mentoring teacher. She suggested that if I apply for my transitional certification, she can help me get on the supply list. That way I can get paid to substitute while I'm finishing out my fourteen weeks of classroom experience."

"Oh! That's great."

"Yeah. It will mean fewer shifts at the diner. I'll need to figure out childcare for any shifts I take, since it won't be during school hours, but I'll figure it out. Marcus and Gail have been vying for aunt and uncle of the year since they found out they're expecting, so I can probably swing it? It feels so good to be in the homestretch, Saint. Taking my classes all spread out like this and years later than most of my peers has sucked. It's like I'm constantly playing catch up. It will be so nice to just have breathing space."

"I'll bet. Congratulations, Angel. You've worked hard for this." He pats my thigh.

"Yeah." I have. The acknowledgement fills me with a warm glow of pride.

I can make this all work. Get the sort of job I dreamed of as a kid. No more settling for anything to pay the overwhelming pile of bills that seems to stack up around me every time I turn around.

That reminds me of the unknown car repair costs looming over me. I slump into my seat and breathe through the anxiety. I can't change it and I'll get through it one step at a time.

"You okay?"

"Yeah. I'm fine. How are you? You seemed off tonight. Did I do something?"

"I'm—" Saint sighs and rubs at his temples and I get the distinct impression he's about to open up to me, but thinks better of it. That stings. I want him to trust me. To lean on me like our friendship is a two-way street instead of me constantly taking from him with nothing to offer in return. "—sorry about my reaction to the fudge. It was a sweet gesture. I guess a part of me panicked, thinking it was a sign you wanted more than what we have and I don't want our friendship to change."

"Isn't that the nature of any relationship though? I mean, I'm no expert since most of mine crash and burn in spectacular fashion, but people aren't stagnant, so why would our interactions be?"

"I suppose."

"Hey, all I'm saying is, if you think fudge means I want you to get down on one knee and propose, you might be watching too many of Carl's rom-coms."

That gets a bark of laughter out of Saint, but he sobers fast. "No, I haven't been seeing as much of Carl lately. I guess that's got me on edge, realizing that even the best things in life sometimes have to end or change in ways you're not ready for."

"I'm sorry. You two have been through a lot together. I'm sure he still loves you, even if he's making time for new love now."

"You think?"

"I mean, I hope so? Not the same, but I'm pretty sure Meg still loves me, even though she spends every spare minute with her friends and ignoring Owen and me. Teenagers, amiright?"

Saint rolls his eyes. "Sure, but she's a teenager and you're her parent. It's not the same."

"No, I get that. But it's natural for her to figure out how to love her friends and us and dance and all the things she wants in her life. Just like it's normal for adults to figure out how new loves fit with the old ones. So, I figure it's probably similar with Carl? He can love you and make room for this new guy? Assuming you guys are still, like—" I search for the word. Then I recall the web comic Meg and her bestie have been gushing over lately, and how they describe the main relationship. "—like, queer platonic partners."

Saint side-eyes me. "We aren't together."

It's my turn to roll my eyes.

"Label it what you want, but you two love each other. It's clear as day, even if it doesn't look the way society says a relationship should look.

Just like our friendship—" I resist the urge to call it a relationship, using a term that's less likely to make Saint run for the hills "—doesn't fit into a tidy box."

"I suppose." Saint pulls up in front of the community center and puts the car in park.

"Just because things change doesn't mean they have to end." I lean over and kiss his cheek. "Thanks for the ride."

I don't expect him to offer a ride home from here. He's made a point of not interacting with my kids much. And I've been grateful for the separation. I'm not about to let another man break their hearts by walking out on them when my inability to maintain a relationship rears its ugly head.

Somehow, I can't see Saint being the sort of step-parental figure who would throw my kids away along with any relationship between us ending, though. He can still snuggle with his ex-husband, after all. Still, I'm not about to push him for more than he's comfortable offering.

"Want me to wait so I can bring you two home?" Saint's fingers brush my elbow, not quite grabbing me, but getting my attention nonetheless.

"Yeah. If it's not too much trouble?"

"Not at all. You shouldn't have to walk in this weather."

"Thanks, Saint. Let me just go get Owen?" I try to ignore the warm glow of hope his offer ignites in my chest. He's just being a caring friend. But it feels momentous that he opened up to me. And even more, that he's willing to acknowledge our friendship in front of Owen.

"Sure. I'll be here." He smiles at me as I ease the car door shut, afraid to damage the sleek paint of the fancy exterior, even though that's probably ridiculous. Nice as it is, it's still just a car.

Saint's car isn't the only one idling in front of the building, but it's one of the nicest. I make my way inside to the milling throng of waiting parents. It's thinner after the competition team's practice than at the end of the general training sessions, less daunting. I chat with a few other parents as we watch the kids finish up and sort out their gear to bring home.

The kids emerge from the gym in a wave. Owen hugs me and I savor the moment of connection.

"Hey, Mike asked if I can come to his Christmas party, can I?" Owen asks, fixing me with his best begging eyes. Ah, so that explains the un-prompted affection.

"It's awful short notice, bud. When is it?" I want to say yes, but I can't give away Trevor's weekend with the kids.

"Tomorrow at his house. I can go home with him and you can pick me up after. Or I can walk. It's only until nine. And it's not even a school night. Please?"

I purse my lips. I was hoping for some family time before the kids go to Trevor's place for the weekend. He normally gets them Friday evening on his weekends, but since he's taking Monday too, he offered to pick them up Saturday instead. Still, Meg already announced her intention to spend the afternoon with her bestie working on their dance routines. Owen deserves to have a good time too.

"Sure. Tell him it's fine."

"Yes! Thanks, Pop. You're the best!" Owen pumps his fist in the air and turns to find his friend in the chaos. I can probably finagle a last-minute shift at the diner while he's occupied. There were dozens of swap requests posted by the schedule last I checked. At least if I'm working, I won't be sitting around missing the kids.

I catch Mike's mom's eye as the boys excitedly discuss their plans. I heft Owen's bag and make my way toward them.

"Hey, how's it going?" I ask Helen.

"Wonderful. Stressed about the party tomorrow, but you know how these things are." She laughs, a tinkling, sweet sound to mask the stress.

"Sure," I force a laugh. I don't have much experience throwing fancy holiday parties, but I've pulled my hair out over putting together birthday parties for the kids, so that's probably close enough.

"Mike is thrilled that Owen can make it. Are there any food issues we should know about?"

"No, he eats everything." I try not to grimace at just how much of everything he's been eating lately. I swear the kid grows an inch every time I turn around and he's only ten. We're going to need to replace his tae kwon do pads by the end of the season if he keeps up at this rate.

"Boys, right?" Helen chuckles and I recall Mike has two older brothers at the high school with Meg. Helen smiles fondly at Owen and Mike with their sweaty heads together as they enthuse about their plans for tomorrow. "Just wait until they're teenagers."

"Yeah." I force a tight smile. I don't want to wish away any time with my kids. Hopefully, I'll be in a better position financially in a few years when Owen is a teenager. "Does he need to bring anything for tomorrow?"

"Oh, no, dear." She gives me the sort of pitying look I've learned to ignore from the parents of my kid's friends. That's the problem with staying in Elk's Pass all my life. Some days, it seems like everyone knows all about me. "If he's got a red or green sweater, we usually have a festive dress code, but I'm sure Mike has an extra one Owen can borrow if need be."

"Okay, thanks. I'll pick him up around nine then?"

"Oh, he's welcome to spend the night. The party usually goes late and Mikey is so excited to have a friend his own age there this year."

"If you're sure it's no trouble?"

"Of course not. Owen is always a pleasure to have over. He'll call you Saturday morning when they're up and ready."

"As long as Owen's ready by ten. He has plans with his other father." I wrap up the conversation with Helen and turn toward Owen. "Hun, our ride is waiting. You'll see Mike tomorrow."

"Yeah, okay, Pop." Owen continues to chatter with his friend, but they both mosey toward the door. So I take Owen's stuff and follow the boys out to the parking lot. Helen guides Mike to her van and Owen waves before scuffing his battered sneakers through the snow behind me. I bite my tongue on a rebuke. His shoes are going to be soggy tomorrow if he keeps that up. Should have made him switch to his boots instead of carrying them for him.

"Whoa!" Owen stops when I guide him to the side of Saint's car. He casts wide eyes between me and the Mercedes. "Dude! Did we get a new car? Sick Christmas present!"

"No, *dude*, we did not get a new car. You remember my friend Saint?"

"Uncle Carl's husband?"

"His ex-husband." I say, weirdly defensive about the correction. Why? It's not like Carl's relationship with Saint somehow invalidates whatever we've got between us. I'm just acting insecure.

Friends. Saint is my friend. My very good friend who spent the past hour sucking me off and is now smiling at my kid as he rolls down the window.

"Everything alright?" Saint asks.

"Yeah." Owen shrugs, saying for Saint to hear, "Except they're always together still. It's kind of weird. You and Dad aren't like that."

"Your father and I aren't the best example of how exes should behave, Owen. Saint, can you pop the trunk for this?" I heft Owen's gear bag. Saint pushes a button and the rear hatch opens.

"So cool!" Owen says. "I like your car, Uncle Saint. Pop says you're giving us a ride home?"

"I am. Your pop's car was having some trouble."

"Ugh, again? Pop, I don't want to take the bus tomorrow!" Owen scowls and stomps his foot in the snow.

"Why not?" I wrestle his bag carefully into Saint's trunk.

"Only little kids take the bus. It's embarrassing," Owen whines. I don't point out that he's certainly acting like a little kid about this.

"Well, you can wake up early and walk or try to get a ride with your sister and Vic," I shoot back, exasperated. Vic's older sister has her license and a car, so she sometimes takes Meg to school in the mornings. She's also the one giving Meg a ride home tonight. "Get in, let's not keep Mr. Saint John waiting."

Owen rolls his eyes at me, but he gets in the car, running eager fingers over the buttery soft leather interior, faux wood panels, and chrome accents. I can empathize with his interest. Everything about the car feels expensive and luxurious when I'm used to bare bones. I get back into the passenger seat next to Saint and turn to shoot my son a quelling look over my shoulder. If he fucks up Saint's car, I'm going to be mortified.

"This is so cool!" Owen crows, finding the button for his heated seats. "Pop, his car toasts your buns!"

Saint stifles a snort, turning it into a cough.

"Buckle up," I demand, suiting actions to words and trying not to flush at the thought of what else Saint has done to my buns. Saint pats my thigh and I don't react to the brief intimacy, but I know Owen notices.

There's something strange in Owen's voice when he says, "Sure, Pop."

Hopefully, it's just that he's not used to seeing me with another adult who shows me open affection like that. I ignore the pang of loss at not getting to show him that. But at least I showed him not to stick around with someone who doesn't respect him, right? Years too late, but I can't bring myself to truly regret the choices that gave me Owen and Meg.

"What time do you have to be at school in the morning, kiddo?" Saint cuts through the silence.

"Eight fifteen." Owen perks up, sensing a treat in the offering.

"Hmm, I could probably swing by on my way to the office and give you a ride to school, if it's okay with your pop."

"Seriously? That would be wicked cool! Pop, can I?" Owen hits me with the puppy-dog eyes. Damn, I love the kid.

I can't say no without being the villain, but this isn't like what Saint pulled with Meg. No calculated manipulation. Just a kind offer of support. Right? Except I'm not sure what it means, or if Saint is really alright with this. Why does everything always have to be so complicated?

"Are you sure? We're out of your way," I hedge.

"I'm sure. I can give you a ride into town too, if you need it."

Yeah, I need it. Except I have to be at the diner by five for the opening shift. Normally, with early shifts, I run home to get the kids out the door for school on what's ostensibly my lunch break. When they were younger, I brought them with me. That way I could feed them breakfast at work before sending them off for the day. Meg is fairly self-sufficient these days and Owen mostly just needs a bit of prompting to remember his lunch and get out the door. It's not like I'm gone for even as long as Barb when she storms out mid-rush for a smoke break.

"What?" Saint asks, glancing at me when I don't respond fast enough.

"Pop's shift starts at the butt crack of dawn," Owen pipes in helpfully.

Great. Butt cracks are just what I want to be thinking of right now, when Saint is being so damn helpful I could swoon. Or run for cover because I am not going to fall for this illusion that I can have it all: my career goals within reach, my kids thriving, and a partner—*friend*—who picks up the slack for me when I need him? Too good to be true.

"Ah, you don't want to get me out of bed? That's sweet, but the roads are slippery and it's supposed to snow so visibility might be poor. Let me give you a ride, Angel?"

I sigh, resigned. "Sure. Far be it from me to refuse a ride from you."

Saint shoots me a look that's equal parts filthy promises of things to come the next time he has me alone, and stern admonishment to behave myself for now. I'm all aflutter from the combination of heat and longing and out of my depth because I don't know how to flirt in front of my kid. This is uncharted territory and I *will not* let that make me sad or guilty.

We discuss logistics for Saint to give me a ride to work and drop off Owen in the morning. I remember to text my boss that I'm available to pick up another shift for tomorrow evening. Since there's a ton of time-off requests logged around the holidays, I'm sure there's someone who would be thrilled to trade with me.

We pull up outside the ramshackle apartment the kids and I have been calling home for years. As part of the divorce settlement, we sold the modest house Trevor and I shared. My share of the sale has helped us to stay afloat, but that little nest egg is all but gone now.

Looking at the saggy front steps and weathered siding through Saint's eyes is uncomfortable. I don't want him to judge me.

"Home, sweet apartment." I force a smile. "You ready, Owen?"

"Yeah." He unbuckles. "Thanks for the ride, Uncle Saint. See you tomorrow!"

"See you, Owen." Saint replies. He glances over to check that Owen is turned away, going to the rear of the vehicle to collect his bag.

Saint leans over to capture my lips in a gentle kiss. His tongue flicks into my mouth, giving me the barest hint of gingerbread and sweetness. He tried the fudge? Saint accepted my gift. For some reason, that has my insides all fluttery.

Does that hint of spice mean he wants to accept that he's important to me? Can that be enough for me? I'm probably reading too much into things. It's just—I don't want our routines to change, but I care about him.

"Pop! The trunk won't open." Owen's call has me pulling away from Saint. He chuckles and hits the button to open the rear.

"He's impatient like his pop," Saint teases me.

"Hardy har," I shove at Saint's shoulder, steal one more peck on his cheek, and get out to let Owen inside. Saint's not wrong, my kid is impatient. I lean in through the open door, drawing out our goodbye as long as I dare. "See you tomorrow. Thanks for the ride, Saint."

"You're welcome. And thanks for the lovely evening and delicious fudge, Angel."

His car idles in front of the building until Owen and I are inside. A lifetime ago, my dad used to wait like that, to be sure I made it where I was going safely. It's been so long since anyone cared about me that much. It's terrifying to think I might be getting used to that kind of care again.

"Hey, Pop?" Owen asks as we're approaching our door at the end of the dingy hallway.

"Yeah, Owen?" I hold my breath, braced for anything he might say.

"Is Saint the reason you're always so happy on Thursdays?" he asks with all the guileless innocence a ten-year-old can muster.

I freeze, unsure of how to answer. It's complicated and I don't want him to say anything tomorrow that will give Saint the wrong idea. But I don't lie to my kids.

"Yeah, buddy. He's a really good friend."

"Your best friend?" Owen presses.

"Yeah."

"Like me and Mikey? Or more like Hannah's mom and her new step-dad?"

"Why do you ask?"

"Because, if it's like Hannah's mom. You can kiss him in front of me. I'm not a baby or anything." Ah. So he saw the kiss. And he seems okay with it.

"That's good to know. Thanks, Owen."

"Hey, Pop?"

"Yes, Owen?"

"Do you think his car can do that thing where it can park itself?"

I laugh, ruffling his sweaty hair. "I'm not sure, bud. You can ask him tomorrow."

"Cool. It would be awesome if he'll let me drive it when I'm older. What's for dinner?"

And just like that, he's off on a tangent and we're back to our usual evening routine. Dinner and homework and squabbling with Meg about what to watch on the TV before bed when she gets home from visiting with her friends after dance. But Owen's right, I'm smiling more than usual as I play chef, tutor, and referee.

Chapter 11

Saint (December 22nd, 2023)

Owen is sitting on the rickety front steps when I pull up in front of Angel's apartment the Friday morning before Christmas. Damn, the place looks even more rundown in the light of day. The kid lights up with a bright smile and slings his bag over his shoulder at the sight of my car.

I wave to him and he runs up to open the passenger side front door. Angel warned me about this.

"Hey, backseat, Owen." I greet him, pointing over my shoulder.

"Pop told you?" He sighs dramatically and gets in the back.

"Yep. I'm afraid so. They also told me your sister has her own ride. So it's just us, right?"

"Yeah."

"You have everything, lunch, homework?"

Owen rolls his eyes at me. "There's no homework; it's the day before vacation. We're going to watch dumb kids' movies and eat cupcakes and stuff. Mrs. Gray is having a party, and then I'm going to Mikey's for his family's party."

"Were you supposed to bring cupcakes or snacks?" I ask.

Angel didn't mention that. Owen fidgets with his seat belt and won't meet my gaze.

"I didn't bring home the signup sheet because it would have stressed Pop out, and it's not like it's a big deal. There will be plenty of cookies and stuff."

"But you want to bring something?"

Owen shrugs.

I think back to my own long-ago class parties, but it's hard to recall. Carl's niece mentioned something about getting juice boxes for her class the last time we visited, I think? Or those little two-bite brownie things she likes. "We could stop at Loblaw's and grab some brownies or juice boxes? I need to stock up on holiday treats for my staff anyway."

"You do?"

Not at all, but my receptionist and part-time paralegal will both appreciate the gesture. And I like the little frosted sugar cookies they have in the bakery this time of year.

"I do," I say.

Angel's son trusts only a little easier than they do. But his narrow gaze softens, and he nods.

"Okay. Brownies would be cool. No nuts, though. Or grapes?"

"We can get both," I offer.

I drive the kid to the store while we compare favorite holiday treats. Once we get there, I'm tempted to pile up a cart with everything he trails his fingers over in the aisle with all the colorful packages of cookies and juice. I restrain that impulse to getting a few things for his party and my office. As we're leaving the store, Owen's stomach grumbles. Angel has mentioned what a bottomless pit the kid has been lately. So I swing through the Tim's drive-through for a second breakfast for him and coffee for myself.

He devours his breakfast sandwich before we pull back onto the road and I hand him my hash browns.

"Thanks." Owen takes the food.

"No problem, kiddo. You must be getting ready for a growth spurt or something."

"I guess. That's what Pop keeps saying." Owen eats another few bites, washing them down with hot cider. Like his pop. It's kind of adorable seeing all the shared mannerisms play out in my rearview mirror. "Hey, Saint?"

"Yeah?"

"Are you being nice to me because you like my pop?"

"Huh?"

"Nothing. Just, you didn't have to get me breakfast. Pop made sure I had food before they left for work."

"I know your pop takes good care of you, Owen."

Owen nods emphatically. "Yes. So, *do* you like my pop?"

"Why are you asking?" It would be easy to like Angel's kids. To get close to their family and twine our lives together, but the hope sparkling in Owen's eyes makes me nervous. I can't envision a world where the wide-eyed kid in the backseat relies on me as anything resembling a parental figure. And yet, a closer relationship with Angel would mean scenes like this would become routine. I don't think I'm equipped for that.

"Because they like you and I don't want them to be lonely on Christmas. So if you like them too, maybe you could spend it together?"

"We'll see, kiddo." I bite my cheek so I don't react to the kid unsubtly playing matchmaker. I turn onto the street where the elementary school's fenced-in yard is full of milling students. Almost home free. "But I'm aromantic, as in I don't experience romantic attraction. You know, like all the hearts and flowers and mushy Valentine's Day card stuff that grown-ups do. I don't date. So it's not like I'm going to be your new step-dad, or anything. Your pop knows that. We're friends."

"Yeah, but I saw you kissing Pop last night. So you're kissing friends."

"Does that bother you?"

"No. I like when Pop is happy." Owen considers me, like he's searching for what Angel sees in me. Damn, the kid knows how to make a guy sweat.

"I like that too." I flash him my most winsome smile. It's nothing short of the truth.

Owen cocks his head to the side. He fixes me with a stern look that forces me to bite my tongue, or risk laughing at how much he resembles his pop when Angel gets peeved with me. "Dad says you're only sleeping with Pop because they owe you money and Pop has daddy issues. But you don't have kids, so I'm not sure what he meant."

Fuck. Can I just punt the kid into the drop-off line and leave? No. I need to address that. Somehow. Probably without expletives about his shithead father.

Ugh. If I had any doubts that I'm not cut out to be a boyfriend, let alone a step-parent, here's all the proof I needed.

"Angel is my very dear friend, Owen. What we do or do not do together is private and between us. But I can assure you that I care about your pop and nothing about our relationship is transactional. And your father probably meant that I'm older than Angel."

"Oh. I guess so. Weird. Why does he care? You're all old." Owen dismisses our respective ages with a wave of his hand. "What's transactional? Pop is trans. Is it something about that?"

"No. That's a fancy way of saying he thinks our friendship is about money or exchanging favors. Your pop doesn't owe me anything; we just enjoy spending time together."

"Pop says you bought Meg's new phone." Owen points out.

I resist the urge to facepalm. Who knew ten-year-olds are experts at cross-examination? "Yeah. But that was a gift, not a transaction."

"Oh." Owen considers.

I gaze longingly at the front of the interminable drop-off line for our turn to get me off the hot seat. The cars ahead of us are crawling. Most of the kids streaming toward the school have various snacks or grocery bags with them. I'm glad we stopped at the store, even if we are cutting it close on time as a result.

"So, did you get me a gift too?" He bats his eyes at me.

I do laugh at that, and wink cheekily at the kid. "That would be telling. You'll have to wait until Christmas to know for sure."

"Boo. Pop says we can't open presents until we get home from Grandma's house."

"I'm sure it will be worth the wait."

"I guess."

Traffic creeps ahead and I'm in the drop-off zone as the school bell rings. Finally.

"Have a great holiday, Owen. Tell your pop I'm looking forward to seeing them again."

"Okay. Thanks for the snacks, Uncle Saint." Owen gathers up his schoolbag, lunch box, and the bags with the snacks we picked for his class.

"Any time, kiddo."

I wait until he's inside the fence, chattering excitedly to a kid in a floppy santa hat before inching back into traffic. I catch Owen pointing at my car. The two boys wave. I raise my hand in acknowledgement before making my way toward my office, head still reeling from a conversation with a kid. That puts into perspective just how big of a raging inferno I've been playing with by falling for Angel these past couple of years. Is it any wonder I'm feeling the heat under Owen's scrutiny?

When this thing between Angel and me was nothing but casual post-divorce rebound sex, that was one thing. But we're actual friends now. My typical reservations about what we've been doing now reach beyond being aro and moderating expectations and into whether I'm cut out to be a parental figure. That was never something I saw in my cards.

I care about Angel. Enough to let them go so they can find someone who treats them like the treasure they are. Someone who can field Owen's incisive questions and promise to always put him and his pop and sister first. My chest squeezes too tight as I accept that fact. It might crush my heart into a pulverized pulp to end things with Angel, but that someone isn't me.

Chapter 12

ANGEL (DECEMBER 22ND, 2023)

I SHIVER IN THE parking lot after my breakfast shift as I watch my brother poke at my car's guts. After practically a lifetime working on the family farm, Marcus knows how to keep any vehicle running. I trust his mechanical expertise. My heart sinks when he slams the hood shut with a grim frown on his face. He scrubs his hands on an old rag that he tucks into his back pocket and shakes his head.

"Sorry, Angel, it's going to need a new engine, this one is cracked and I'm pretty sure the catalytic converter is on its way out too. It would cost more in new parts than we could get selling it for scrap."

"Fuck." I tug at my hair, trying to estimate how much this is going to cost me.

I've known my vehicle was on its last legs for years, but did the damn thing really have to die days before Christmas? My boss might have been understanding last night, but he won't let me leave the car here indefinitely. A tow is going to cost me dearly. Besides, I don't know where to store it when our building's lot has a strict snow removal schedule, so it can't sit there forever either.

Let alone, how do I even begin going about getting rid of the thing? I kick the damn car's tire, taking out all the anger and frustration that I can't ever seem to get ahead, even a little, no matter how hard I try. The surge of adrenaline makes me just want to keep kicking until something breaks.

Marcus puts his hands on my shoulders and squeezes. I tense at first, but then relax into his touch when he starts shushing me.

"Hey, it's alright, little si—sibling." He stutters over what to call me, but corrects himself mid-syllable, and I can tell he's trying. I'm just thankful he's here with me. Making the effort to connect as he rocks me from side to side. "I can help get it hauled out of here and make the arrangements to sell it. I can even hook you up with one of the old trucks from the farm."

Arms crossed over my chest, I spin to glare at my brother. "I'm not accepting a new car from you."

Marcus snorts. "Fine, it's a truck, and it's far from new. But listen, Gail and I have been talking, and I owe you a proper apology. When I graduated from high school, our folks helped me with school and gave me the Tahoe to drive there. When you graduated..."

"They kicked me out."

"Yeah." Marcus runs an engine-grease stained hand through hair and blows out a noisy breath. "Exactly. It was wrong, but I couldn't afford to pay your tuition or give you a car back then. So I thought it wasn't my fault, but now that I'm in a position to help you, I want to pass along something. And I didn't want to say anything at the time, because I didn't want to rub salt in the wounds. It wasn't in my control to change anything. Our folks put the money from Gran's inheritance into a trust for when I had a kid. They want us to use it to start a university fund, but Gail and I have full financial discretion once we get access to the trust. So when Trace is born, we'll be coming into some money. Gail and I want to split it with you. Half and half."

I stare at my brother in mute incomprehension. I don't know what to say. Gran was in a nursing home recovering from a stroke when my folks cut me out. Since they had control of her visitors, they cut me off from her too. She died of a second stroke before Meg was born. I never expected so much as a photograph from her after how that all went down. I was just glad Marcus got me her fudge recipe.

"Say something?" Marcus is staring at me and I can't deal with the remembered grief and anger at being denied a final goodbye.

"Why?"

"Because Gran loved you. She'd have wanted you to have something of hers. Because it's the right thing to do and she would have adored your kids?"

"No. Not that. Why are you suddenly so invested in making shit up to me, Marcus?"

"Because, much as it shames me to admit it, I didn't understand how fucked up what our folks did to you was until recently. And by the time

I moved back to take over on the farm, you were married and expecting Owen, and you seemed happy."

"I wasn't."

"Yeah. I get that *now*. And Meg might have mentioned how much you've been struggling to pay the bills."

Fuck. My stomach sinks. "I didn't put her up to asking you for anything. We'll be fine. I'll be teaching by next fall and things will improve."

Marcus waves me away. "That's the thing, Angel. You're family. You don't have to ask. If you won't accept for your own sake, then let me at least help for my niece and nephew's sake. The farm is as much their birthright as it is mine. And I can afford it."

"I'll pay you back for the truck."

"We can work out an arrangement. And I'm not accepting a no on your share of Gran's money. If you won't take it, then I'll set up RESPs for the kids' education."

"Their grandmother already has education funds for them both."

"So, you can invest the money, or take a vacation, or move out of that shithole you've been renting; it's enough for a nice down payment on a house. Or a newer car. The point is, it's yours to use as you see fit."

"We'll see about that." I shake my head at him. It would be great if we could afford a nicer place. But I don't want to owe Marcus any more than I want to be reliant on anyone else's kindness.

Marcus sighs, dropping the subject. "Are you coming to Eliza and Grace's Christmas party tomorrow?"

"Yeah."

"Good. Eliza and her wife are looking for someone to tutor their daughter, and I might have suggested you."

"I don't offer tutoring."

"I know. But you could. I've seen you with your kids. You're going to be an amazing teacher and I bet Eliza and other parents would pay you well for your personalized expertise."

"Maybe." I bite my lip, giving it serious consideration.

It's weird to think of myself as someone with desirable skills. The praise isn't unwelcome or unwarranted, it's just disconcerting to hear it. From the know-it-all older brother who has a history of making me feel silly and overlooked, no less. But it's been a lifetime since Marcus was the aloof teenager I was desperate to emulate; it might be time to let myself get to know the man he's become. The glimpses I've seen promise that he's worth my time these days.

"Gail was saying they have online platforms that offer it for a pretty penny. It might be a good side hustle to consider. You know, if you're going to be stubborn about accepting help."

"I'll consider it."

"Good." Marcus nods, like that settles the matter. Maybe it does. It's not like I haven't considered the idea before, but it seemed overwhelming and the more reputable places wanted credentials I didn't have yet. But now that I've got my provisional license, there are a bunch of online platforms that I might be eligible for. It's worth looking into again, when I have the time.

I notice Barb approaching the door to the diner and curse under my breath. This took longer than I'd hoped.

"I've got to get back inside. My next shift is about to start."

"Sure, I'll take care of getting this junker hauled away. I can leave the truck here for you by the end of the night. We've been using it for tree deliveries, but today is the last day we're offering that service."

"Ah, so it might smell like Christmas?" I joke. Good thing almost a month of having one of his beloved trees in our living room has mostly inured me to the melancholy that once-familiar scent has invoked for years.

"Yep, holiday fresh, all year long." Marcus nudges our shoulders together. "I'll have Gail run the keys in to you later?"

"Yeah, that would be good. Look up the Blue Book value and I'll pay you."

"It's ancient. I'll take $1200 in monthly payments, spread over the next two years."

I scowl at him. "You're being ridiculous."

"Fine, throw in the clunker and I can knock it down by half."

"Marcus!"

"Seriously, I'll get an okay rate selling your old car for scrap. It's a reasonable trade."

"Fine. Deal." We shake, and Marcus pulls me into a hug.

"I know you're used to being on your own, but I want to be a better brother and uncle to you and your kids, Angel. Please don't be a stranger?"

"Yeah. I'll try. Thanks, Marcus."

A cynical part of me is still upset that it took his wife going through a rough pregnancy to wake up to what I went through alone. I needed my big brother and he wasn't there. But he's genuinely been doing his best to make up for that lately.

It's not fair to hold our parents' sins against him. I sure as shit didn't advertise how miserable I was in my marriage with Trevor. Marcus isn't the most socially aware guy, so I can either continue holding the past against him or build a better relationship with my brother now.

I'm glad we're reconnecting. I like Marcus's wife and her family a lot. It will be nice to hold his baby in a few months, breathe in that sweet newborn smell and fall in love with my niece. It doesn't hurt that I'll get to hand her back to her parents at the end of each visit.

The baby years are hard. I don't precisely want to go back, but I like the idea of having a new baby in the family. As long as there is another adult to hand them off to when I'm exhausted.

And it helps that a small part of me likes the fact Gail gives me another connection to Saint through her brother. A way to touch other parts of his life outside the bedroom without scaring him off. Or at least, I hope so.

I'm looking forward to seeing Saint at the party tomorrow. Better to look forward to that than to spend my entire night dreading saying Merry Christmas to the kids before packing them off to their dad's place for the holiday. Our first one apart.

I'm grateful not to have the time to dwell on that fact as I go back inside to a packed lunch service that keeps me running from start to finish.

Chapter 13

SAINT (DECEMBER 23RD, 2023)

"DANCE WITH ME?" ANGEL looks radiant in an oversized, slouchy sweater and tight jeans. Their long hair is pulled back into a tidy tail with a festive light-up scrunchie. They're smiling, but I can see the traces of sadness in their eyes whenever their gaze falls on the several children and teens in attendance.

It's obvious they miss Meg and Owen already, and that they want a distraction.

"Sure." I flash them a tight smile. Angel guides me into the little knot of people dancing to the holiday music while most of the other guests mingle and snack on hors d'oeuvres.

So far, I've spent most of the night lurking at the edges of the crowd and feeling sorry for myself that Carl is having an amazing time with Nick. And working really hard not to resent my bestie's new boyfriend for monopolizing his time.

The goofy grin that hasn't slipped from Carl's face once all evening has gone a long way to assuaging my jealousy. As long as Carl is smiling like that, I'm a fan of this Nick. But I have my doubts. For a start, this is the first time in years that the man has come home to spend the holiday with his aging mother.

Nick seems nice enough. I'm just wary of his priorities. Carl deserves the very best, not to settle for another workaholic like me who can't give him what he needs from a lover. But so far, they seem perfect for each other. It's good. And so is holding Angel close and swaying to the music.

"Do you remember the first time I asked you to take me home?" Angel murmurs.

I have to stoop to hear them. I catch a glimpse of Nick alone with Eliza's wife, Grace. Hmm, I wonder what Eliza has planned? Carl's sisters are nosy as fuck, god love them.

"Mhm." I flash Angel a distracted smile as I turn us in a spin, casually sweeping the room for Eliza and Carl. Angel's smile dims, their expression closing off. "What?"

"Nevermind." They stop dancing.

I remember that night like it was yesterday. The warmth of their body in my arms. The thrill of taking them home and unwrapping them like a much anticipated present. My excitement when they agreed to see me again. I remember how we danced, just like this.

Their hair—silky when it brushes over my hand on their shoulder—was shorter then, and equally gorgeous. They'd buzzed it all off to celebrate their separation from Trevor and starting hormones once they were free of their old life. So a couple years out from that, it had just brushed their shoulders in an awkward rockstar do, and it's longer now. Their smile that night drew me to them, and I could kick myself for banishing it.

"I remember, Angel." I don't want to reminisce like we're lovers. Even though, aren't we? I *do* love them. But it's never the right way and I'm so tired of losing people when they realize it never will be something out of one of Carl's romances. That he'll always be my—what was that word Meg taught Angel for queer platonic life partners? An aubergine? No, zucchini. I'll have to ask the kid if us old folks are allowed to use that one. It's what Carl is to me, though. The one I want to grow old loving, having movie nights and gym dates together. I want to live beside him until we're the cranky old men telling the neighborhood kids to get off our lawns.

Except, maybe Carl and Nick—or whoever he ends up with—will be those kids' grandparents. And maybe I'll be something to Angel's grandkids too. If I can figure out how to be something to them and their kids.

The thought gives me a visceral reaction, a hot flush I don't know how to quantify. Fear? Excitement? Some rancid combination of the two? I have no idea how to be a partner to Angel. Let alone a step-parent to their kids.

"Cool. Is everything okay?" Angel looks concerned. They lift the back of their hand to my brow in such a parental gesture that I almost laugh. I'm the furthest thing possible from one of their kids, but it's a painfully loving touch. I can't tell them the reason I've broken out in a flop sweat is that I'm having a mild panic attack about getting to know their kids.

"Yeah." There's Carl, by the punch. And from his fidgeting and the 'save me' eyes he's casting in my direction, he needs an extraction. Yep, Carl needs me. I'm not fleeing in terror of the future at all. "Of course."

"You sure? You seem distracted." Angel follows me as I wend my way across the room.

"A little. Sorry. Look, there's your brother. Can we catch up later?"

"Sure, Saint. I need to talk with Grace anyway." Angel doesn't quite storm off in a huff, but they don't seem happy either.

Carl keeps looking over at Nick. Ah. So it isn't me who he wants to rescue him. Well, I can still help nudge that along. I change course. Marcus is standing near Nick and Grace now. I cringe internally when I notice Angel is also closing in on the little group.

Well, if Nick needs a push to make Carl happy, that's one job I can be the right man for. Then I can make it up to Angel without giving them the wrong idea about what we are to each other.

"Seems like Carl is looking for you." I nudge Nick's elbow without pretext. He gives me a bemused smile, then excuses himself to go rescue Carl from his sister's interrogation. Mission accomplished.

I lurk at the edge of the conversation between Grace and Angel, like a creeper. Something about tutoring Grace's daughter. Angel would be good at that. If their obligations didn't already have them spread paper-thin. I bite back my objections. It's not up to me to micromanage their life choices. Friends support each other.

Angel seems engaged in their conversation with Marcus and Grace and soon the three of them are in full-on parent mode, talking about their kids. From the snippets I overhear, I'm not sure if Grace and Angel are reminiscing about their kids as babies or trying to terrify Marcus. Either way, I don't envy what his near future has in store with his firstborn due in the spring.

Either way, it only drives home how woefully unprepared I am to be what Angel needs in a partner. How many zucchinis are you allowed to have, anyway? And can you fuck them?

Agh. Questions that I probably shouldn't text to Meg. She'd probably laugh at the first one. The second one is absolutely not for her eyes, though. Even if she's all but spelled out that she knows what's between me and her pop.

It's probably weird that despite enjoying my talks with Meg and Owen when we've interacted, the abstract idea of having a formal role in their lives sends me into a panic. Becoming a parent does not compute, but being friendly to my friend's snarky teenager and earnest pre-teen is easy. Could that be enough?

I dance with Angel again, and this time we don't talk. We just sway to soft holiday crooning until Eliza cuts the sound system to gather everyone together for the ornament swap. My time to shine. I wait eagerly as we get organized, and everyone who brought an ornament draws a numbered Christmas ball from an oversized Santa hat. Eliza goes all out for this stuff.

I get number three, so I probably won't end up going home with whatever I unwrap. Since everyone has the choice to keep what they pick from the tree or trade it for whichever already opened ornament they want, trades are common.

Angel gets twenty-five. The last choice means they'll get their pick of all the ornaments, perfect. They deserve something nice. On my turn, I pluck a candy-cane striped gift bag from the ornament tree and pull out a generic porcelain angel.

It's cheap quality and probably mass-produced and I normally wouldn't give it a second glance, except the long dark hair and inquisitive expression remind me of my Angel. I want to keep it. Hold it in my heart and remember the gorgeous person throwing me glances from across the circle forever, even if I can't see how we can work long term.

I hold my breath every time someone glances my way, but round after round passes and no one takes away my angel. The ornament I brought—a locally hand-crafted felt gnome with a rainbow hat and a tiny Christmas tree slung over his shoulder—causes a stir when Carl picks it to open.

"My mom made that!" Nick crows excitedly.

"And I brought it!" I lift my cup of punch in triumph. "That's the winning ornament, mark my words."

"We'll see about that. Mine is going to give you a run for your money," Marcus teases as he salutes me with his drink.

"This still isn't a competition, Saint," Carl says with a groan that can't hide his bemused smile.

"Then explain how I've won it five years running," I shoot back. "Last year with Oliver was a fluke that doesn't count."

"He has a point, Carl." Eliza has a long history as a shit-stirrer. "Saint always brings the most coveted ornament."

"You're impossible." Carl sips his punch, but Nick tugs him to sit in his lap.

"He's also right. Give it." Gail makes grabby hands as she trades the pretty silver bell she just opened for the gnome. Carl pouts, not wanting to give it up, but he relents in the end.

"The rules are the rules," Eliza chides him.

"I told you it's a winner," I joke, raising my glass to Carl. I keep my little porcelain angel tucked quietly out of sight so as not to draw any would-be ornament trader's attention.

Sure enough, the adorable gnome I contributed to the game makes his way around the circle, getting chosen half a dozen times in as many rounds. My reign as the champion ornament picker is secure for another year. Excellent.

And then Angel takes down the last ornament, a jolly little Santa who resembles one of the gaudy numbered balls we used to determine turn order.

They smirk at me, stroking their chin as they play up pondering the choice. "Hm, I'm thinking I should take that angel from Saint. That seems fitting. An angel for Angel and Saint Nick for a Saint."

"In that case, you should give it to Nick," Carl pipes in, noticing my reflexive grip tightening on my angel and trying to shield me from having to surrender it. From the perplexed look on his face, he has no idea why I'm so attached to the plain little thing. Normally, I'd have done everything in my power to encourage someone to trade it away from me. But not this time.

Angel considers, glancing between the Santa, my angel ornament and the rainbow-coiffed gnome in Nick's grasp. "Alright, looks like I'll take the winning ornament then. Give it, Nick!"

Nick makes the trade, playing up a loud groan at being made to surrender the most popular ornament. I'm starting to really like that guy. He's making my two favorite people smile, playing along in our games.

"Looks like Saint remains the champion of ornament swap." Eliza observes with a cheeky grin.

"Somehow, considering it's not an actual competition," Carl gripes, but it's all for show. He's smiling fondly at me from Nick's lap. I could get used to seeing him that happy.

"Who's ready for some more eggnog?" Grace breaks up the circle of guests. Next, they'll have Grace's dad make a grand entrance dressed as Santa to distribute gifts to all the kids, and things will wrap up for the night shortly afterward.

I carefully tuck my ornament back into the gift bag it came in for safekeeping and go to peruse the dessert buffet for a few more cookies.

"Hey, can we get our ride home a bit early?" Carl snags my sleeve to ask as I'm scanning the crowd and plotting out my goodbyes.

I offered to be his and Nick's designated driver. Although as far as I can tell, Nick hasn't had more than a few sips of butter rum when we first arrived all night. That's a crying shame, considering how delicious Eliza's butter rum is.

Next year I'll indulge. Or I might call to get her recipe tomorrow. I always mean to, but then I forget in all the hubbub. I don't have anywhere to be until after the holiday now, so it's the perfect year to try my hand at making the rich, sugary-sweet drink.

"Yeah, I was just thinking it's about that time. Everything alright?"

"Mhm," Carl hums, tight-lipped, and I get the distinct impression it's really not, but I don't pry in front of a crowd. I can see Nick pacing near the door as he texts frantically. "Nick needs to make a work call."

"Ah. Sure, get your coats. Give me a minute to say a few good nights." I purse my lips in disapproval and I have to remind myself that Carl likes Nick. Still, I barely refrain from saying anything disparaging.

"Yeah, you do." Carl cuts his gaze toward Angel. I'm not surprised he noticed the tension between us. Even if he appears to be misreading it. I'm not sure how to feel about Angel right now, but I've sent them enough mixed signals for one night.

Sometimes, I wish my friendships could be as straightforwardly embraced as the romantic relationships that always get lionized everywhere I look. It's so frustrating to know everyone will expect me to step back from my role in Carl's life if Nick asks it of him. And the town gossip mill would probably side with Angel if I break their heart by not reciprocating the growing feelings I've been pretending not to notice from them. I'm too tired and cranky to deal with my own anticipatory grief, bracing for my two most important friendships to change. All because of love. Phooey on that nonsense.

I make a point of wishing Eliza and Grace's kid a happy holiday. The kid calls me Uncle, so she gets a greeting. I say goodnight to her parents too. Then I duck into the spare bedroom to grab my coat ahead of the end of the party rush. Carl and Nick are already waiting for me outside; I saw them leave.

I'm surprised when I turn and almost run right into Angel in the hallway.

"Hey," I say, trying to hide my guilt over my attempt to sneak off without a proper goodbye.

"Hey, yourself." Angel hugs themself, looking insecure. "Are we still on for Christmas?"

"Yeah, text me?" I could kick myself for the dismissive answer. They clearly need reassurances, but it would be worse to offer them platitudes when I'm not sure if I can keep doing what we're doing, right? At least this way, it's not out of left field.

"Okay. You just seemed weird tonight. If I did something…" Angel rubs at their arms, self-soothing.

"No." I'm not going to let that stand. Angel didn't do a damn thing to deserve this. I'm just not built for relationships. And lately, that seems like it includes friendships. "You didn't do anything wrong. Carl and Nick had something come up. They're waiting for me to take them home. Sorry, I need to go."

"Ah. Right. I should get going too, I guess."

"It is getting late," I agree, even though it's clear from their hopeful gaze that they're fishing for an invite. I understand why they wouldn't want to be alone tonight. A selfish part of me wants to spend the entire weekend curled up in bed with them. But the more responsible side of me realizes that's a terrible idea if I don't want to blur the lines between sex and love.

I love Angel too much to let that happen any more than it already has. This is better for both of us in the long run, even if I'm consigning us both to a lonely Christmas. The hope in their eyes dims and then dies.

"Well, have a good night, Saint." Angel shuffles past me.

"Good night, Angel." I can't resist leaning in to kiss their cheek. They tense at first, but then they turn their face to return the gesture. Their grip on my arm is tight, as if they want to cling to me, but know it's futile.

They're smiling that bittersweet, knowing smile of theirs when I step back. Like they suspect that was more of a goodbye than I'm letting on. Damnation. I don't want it to be, but that might be for the best if I can't get my head out of my ass about them.

That's a problem for another day. I pretend not to see the hurt on Angel's face or the disappointed droop of their shoulders as I leave. I can't shake the sense of their sad eyes boring into my back the entire way to my car with Carl and Nick.

Chapter 14

ANGEL (DECEMBER 24TH, 2023)

I DRINK TOO MUCH after Saint leaves the party at Eliza and Grace's place. My head is throbbing and the unfamiliar floral wallpaper takes me a minute to place when I wake up with a killer hangover. I'm in Marcus's guest bedroom. Not the one they've turned into a nursery, thank fuck. That might have made me think I somehow traveled back in time to when I was expecting Owen and everything was yellow duckies and endless diapers.

And a hellscape of never measuring up to Trevor's expectations and always feeling like an inadequate mother and wife because of how terribly the titles fit me. It didn't matter what I did; it was never right. Never enough.

But I'm not there. I can own the fact that I am the best Pop to my kids I can be, and soon Trevor will barely be a part of my life. I should probably be sad about what that will mean for the kids, but mostly I'm grateful. Better a clean break now than a long, drawn out death by a thousand cuts to their relationship. Better for Owen to realize Trevor has abandoned him in one fell swoop than gradually over dozens more missed weekends and years of broken promises and canceled plans.

I should probably be ashamed to wake up in my brother's guest bed on Christmas Eve morning with only hazy recollections of how I got here. But it is what it is. The last thing about the party that's really clear to me is how Saint brushed me off and the finality of that goodnight kiss. I always knew he was out of my league, but I didn't expect losing him to hurt this much. Or for it to happen when I was already struggling with the holidays.

When I pry myself out of bed and down to the kitchen, Gail is sitting with a cup of tea. Her mug smells like peppermint, and Marcus is cooking pancakes for her.

"Hey, grab a coffee and join us." Marcus gestures to the coffeemaker with his spatula as he scrapes the last of the batter onto a hot griddle. "Gail was craving strawberry pancakes, and I'm making plenty."

At my wince, Gail gives me a sympathetic smile. "There's Tylenol in the cupboard with the mugs."

"Thanks." I force a grateful smile and try not to ache with envy at the sweet way my brother dotes on his wife. What would that have been like? Probably as lovely and comforting as when Saint makes me warm apple cider and rubs my shoulders after a long day at the diner. I shake that thought right out of my head.

Saint isn't my boyfriend, and he told me up front that he doesn't do those big romantic gestures. Except he does all the practical little things that make me feel adored. I don't need flashy declarations and worthless gestures. I just need the steady guy who is there for me and smiles when I indulge his sweet tooth. But he can't seem to accept that and I refuse to chase after what I can't have.

If I had any pride left, I wouldn't text Saint about tonight. It's all too clear we're not still on for our plans, but I don't want to face my first Christmas without my kids alone. How many times did Saint swear he's my friend? Well, I desperately need one tonight.

Even if the benefits part of our friendship is over, and that chaste kiss said it might be, Saint is the only one I want to spend tonight with. Still, it might be better to spend it alone than with someone who is too nice to tell me I outstayed my welcome. My eyes burn at the thought of no more Thursdays with Saint, but I tell myself that's just the hangover making them irritated.

I eat breakfast with Marcus and Gail, then beg off from spending the day with them, claiming my headache as an excuse. Marcus gives me a ride back to Eliza's place to pick up my truck. I have a vague memory of agreeing to tutor Marcus's niece before I got wasted.

Hopefully, I didn't fuck that up already. Grace offered me an hourly rate that almost made my eyes pop out of their sockets. A few regular tutoring clients like that, and I might be able to finally stop living from paycheck to paycheck. No more draining my meager savings with every unforeseen expense and minor emergency.

When I get home, the apartment seems empty as a tomb without Meg and Owen in it. I miss our ancient, bedraggled artificial tree, but it's broken beyond repair. The live one we replaced it with this year makes the entire apartment smell mockingly festive. Today that is back to reminding me sharply of loss.

With the lights dark, it's just a sad beacon of everything I don't have today. How alone I am. No point driving up the utilities by lighting it if the kids aren't home to enjoy it, though. The carefully wrapped presents under the branches only serve to remind me of how alone I am.

I go up to the tree anyway. Face the ghosts haunting me head on. Laminated handprint ornaments from both kids' baby days flutter when I approach. Hard to believe their hands were ever that tiny. I caress the red and green paint. It seems fitting that even that small, comforting piece of them remains separated from me behind a layer of thick protective plastic. I'm being maudlin; they'll be home on Monday with all their exuberant holiday cheer and teenage angst and everything that makes them who they are.

I hang the colorful gnome ornament from the party front and center, near my trans pride flag, Meg's gaudy bisexual cat, and Owen's pirate flag. Those three hang front and center, at eye level.

I bite my lip. This tree is covered in memories. Some small part of me hopes that by putting even a tiny fragment of Saint on it, I can let him have a bigger place in my life. Some mark that he's more than a convenient stress relief. So much more. The gnome, with its bright rainbow hat, seems to mock me, brimming with all the cheer I just can't muster.

I turn my back on the tree and bundle myself into bed to sleep off my hangover. With any luck, things will look brighter when my head isn't throbbing in time with my pulse and I'm not on the verge of puking up my guts.

It's dark when I wake up freezing. Too dark, and too quiet. Not even the low hum of the fridge and all the other electronics that fade into the background until they're gone. I glance at my alarm clock, but the face has gone dark. We lost power. Again. From how much the temperature has dropped, it happened a while ago. Fuck only knows when it will be back with the holiday weekend.

Fuck. I rake my fingers through my hair as I consider my options. Earlier, I figured I should skip pestering Saint about tonight. No sense pushing myself on him when he seemed so lukewarm about our plans last night. But I can't stand to be around Marcus, with the perfect life he's building, and there isn't anyone else I can call.

I don't want to be alone, but I don't want to be around people either. I shiver. Maybe I can just go to my brother's house for a bit to warm up. Except, Marcus won't let me come back to a place with no heat if I can't take being around a happy family all night.

So that leaves Saint. He already invited me over. My phone is on its last dregs of a charge. I could text, but if he doesn't get back to me right away, it might die before I hear from him.

I dial Saint's number before I can chicken out. My pulse pounds as I wait for an answer, mind racing with what I'll do if he rejects me. At least he doesn't send me straight to voicemail or dismiss my call on the first couple of rings.

I wait with bated breath for the chance to blurt out my plea for him to just give me one more night before he ends us. Or even just one night as friends because I need a friend so badly right now. I squeeze the phone as it rings one last time, and the voicemail picks up. No answer. I bite my lip. Consider calling back. Give him one more chance?

Or I could text after all. Try to find somewhere that's open so I can at least charge my phone and grab something for dinner. There's no point even trying to get hold of the property manager. He doesn't take calls on the weekend and his voicemail has been full for as long as we've lived here. It would take an actual flashing sirens type emergency to get him to deal with an issue on Christmas Eve, and even that might not cut it.

I'm staring at the text thread with Saint when my phone rings in my hand. It startles me so much that I almost drop it. My stomach swoops with reignited hope. Saint! That makes me laugh at myself. It's probably an ill-timed telemarketer. Or someone calling about an unpaid bill or...

I answer without bothering to check. "Hello?"

"Hey, Angel, did you still want to come over tonight?"

I almost sob in relief at Saint's timely offer. He must just have missed my call. It's possible I read too much into that goodbye kiss last night. Maybe...

"Carl and I are having a holiday movie marathon, and he thought you might want to get your mind off missing the kids."

Ah. So he wants to make it clear this is a pity thing. For a friend. Fine. I'll take it.

"Yeah. That would be really nice. We lost power here, so I could use a place to stay tonight. If that's still alright?"

"Heat too?" Saint tries to hide his concern, but it warms me to know he still cares, even if he's trying not to show it.

"Yeah."

"Well, pack a bag and come on over. I'm at Carl's place and we're making some comfort food since his boyfriend ditched him last minute for a work emergency."

"Oh, that stinks."

"It sure does. See you soon?"

"I'll be there. Thanks, Saint."

"Don't mention it, Angel. We can—"

My phone cuts out mid-sentence. The screen is completely dark as it chimes its little power off jingle.

Well, good thing Saint offered me somewhere to go for tonight. I'm not going to obsess over what he wanted to do with me—much. I throw a few things into the overnight bag I've been using for our weekend visits. Debate whether to include the gift the kids picked out for him after realizing he got them both the top asks on their wish lists.

I had to tell Owen that the big box under the tree is his new console when Meg got her new phone early, but he's practically been a saint about waiting for the holiday to open it. I hold the gift-wrapped proof that my kids like the man I've been falling for and consider what to do with it, chest tight with emotions I'm not sure how to handle. Saint is definitely being weird with me.

I was just starting to get comfortable with my kids knowing about Saint's place in my life. If I'm honest, I was starting to think I could rely on his friendship to be there for me when I need it. Did he really have to wait until he slipped past all my defenses to get all weirdly distant? Am I going to have to remember him every time Owen plays his new games?

I should pack the gift, I don't want it here to remind me of all the good times—his steady, caring presence in my life—if this is the end of our regular Thursday nights. But I still hesitate, since I wasn't with them,

I'm not sure what the kids got for Saint, just that they asked me to give it to him tonight. It could be anything.

They went shopping with Marcus and Gail, and then again with Trevor's mom at the holiday market a few days ago when she made the hour drive into town. I've always tried to include her in their lives, even when Trevor flakes on their plans. I get along with their grandmother well enough. Better than my nonexistent relationship with my folks. They spend their winters on some beach somewhere, last I heard.

While I dither over the present, I make sure I have everything else I might need, phone charger for sure so the kids can get in touch if they need me. Their gift might make Saint uncomfortable. I'm sure he'll realize it's not trivial for him to make it onto my kids' very limited gift list. On the one hand, I don't want to put that pressure on him, however indirectly. But not letting him know won't change the fact that they got it for him, and they're going to ask me about his reaction.

I stuff the parcel into my bag and make sure that everything is turned off in the apartment in case the power comes back while I'm gone. It's clear what happened to the power as soon as I step outside. Ice encases every bare tree branch and power line in glittering crystals. It was raining earlier, a steady drizzle that melted the festive snow and apparently turned into freezing rain while I was napping. It's treacherous out here, but a part of me is relieved it's not just faulty wiring or something specific to our building again.

I make my way gingerly out to the truck and hop into the driver's seat. Much as I hate taking advantage of Marcus's kindness, it's a relief not praying the engine will actually turn over every time I stick the key in the ignition.

The drive to Saint and Carl's duplex is weirdly quiet, practically no one on the icy streets and all the houses lit up. Well, except the ones on our block where the power outage seems pretty widespread. The rain for most of the day means the snow that was starting to accumulate is mostly a slushy, frozen mess. The icy coating on every surface makes for a starkly different kind of winter wonderland. It would be more wondrous if I didn't know how destructive that much ice can be.

It feels like I'm the only one without a family and a place to be tonight, driving past all the festive homes with cars in their drives. All those other families gathered together around their trees. I know that's far from reality, but it's a lonely few minutes and I second-guess whether Saint even wants me there a thousand times.

I'm still worrying my lip over whether there is anywhere else I can go when Saint opens the door to Carl's place as I walk up the front stairs. Saint takes one look at my face and sweeps me into a hug. And I have a haven here in his arms.

All my doubts and reading into his kiss last night evaporate when Saint holds me. Things between us might change, but I get one more night of his friendship. That's exactly what I need right now.

CHRISTMAS MUSIC AND MOVEMENT wake me from a sound sleep. I take a moment to orient myself. I'm sprawled on Carl's couch, legs across Saint's lap. Saint lies slumped half on top of me. His hand rests lightly on my hip, his cheek nestled against me. There's an empty spot on Saint's other side where Carl was sitting when I fell asleep sometime around three movies into our holiday marathon.

It takes me a moment to realize Carl didn't go up to bed after the movies. He's standing in the front window, looking out at whatever is making the racket that woke us.

"Oh!" Carl exclaims, with all the wonder of a little kid catching Santa's arrival.

Then he claps a hand over his mouth and glances toward the couch, like he doesn't want to wake Saint and me. It's endearing. The sort of moment where I completely understand Saint's protectiveness toward the giant teddy bear of a man.

Carl dashes for the door. I yawn and crane my neck to see what caught his attention. It looks like fresh snow. Brr. I'm plenty cold enough. I contemplate snuggling closer to Saint, but I don't want to wake him. When I glance at his face, he's smiling at me.

"Have a good sleep, Angel?" He reaches to brush the long hair out of my face.

"Yeah." I stretch, yawning widely. "You?"

"Sure. Other than that racket. Shall we see what's going on out there?" Saint rises, gesturing to the window. I nod, watching as Saint crosses to peer outside. His lounge pants are riding low on his hips and the view distracts me from following. "Oh."

I'm not sure how to interpret that flat exclamation, an echo of Carl's earlier, so I walk up behind him and take in the scene. Nick is in front of Carl, singing Christmas carols and... "Is that a snow machine?"

"Yes, it appears to be." Saint shakes his head, but there's a bemused smile on his lips. "The fucker went all out to win him back. Next level apology."

I watch Nick groveling out in the fresh snow. I can't hold back a laugh at the two of them out there. It's like a scene out of the sappy movies Carl loves. I clap a hand over my mouth to cover my reaction. It's totally over the top and ridiculous, but Carl's huge smile says he is devouring every corny drop with gusto.

"That's good, right? This is the sort of romance Carl wants?"

"It is." Saint nods. He's been calling Nick every name in the book for breaking Carl's heart ever since I arrived last night, but he seems to be thawing toward the man now. "We should clear out so they can, uh, make up."

I snort at his delicate wording. "Good call."

We turn toward Carl's front door, missing whatever happens next with the tableau outside between Carl and Nick.

"Um, is it okay if I crash at your place until a decent hour?" It's super awkward to be the one to ask, but I'm not ready to face the echoing emptiness of home, and I'm still tired.

"Sure." Saint slings an arm around my shoulders. He gives me a squeeze and kisses my temple. "Stay until the power is back at your place. Or at least until you have to pick up the kids."

I grab my bag, heart tripping at the thought of bringing my kids back to his place. Sharing the holiday with this man who helps me shoulder my burdens and gives me space to lay them down to rest. That's asking too much though. We let ourselves out to observe quietly as Carl gazes at Nick with stars in his eyes. They kiss under the lightly falling machine-made snow and Carl looks blissful as his boyfriend holds his hand and they turn toward his home as one.

Saint teases him, but Carl takes it in stride. I congratulate the love-birds. It's weird to watch a grand gesture like that from the sidelines. I know it's an expression of love between those two. Nick knew it would delight Carl, and it did. But I don't think I'd be comfortable with that sort of display.

It would feel like an emotional manipulation to me after everything I've been through for years with Trevor. It's a relief knowing without even having to ask that Saint wouldn't put me in that sort of high pressure position.

Is that what he means when he says he doesn't date? That he won't do the sort of grand gesture we just witnessed? Because I'm not sure how to tell him how much I appreciate what we have. I wish I had the words to ask him for more. Not more *than* what we have now. More *of* us. More nights in his bed. More texts. More time.

Saint shepherds me into his house and I let myself enjoy having his arm around me, possessing but not possessive.

"Bed or breakfast?" Saint asks through a yawn. He scratches idly at his belly and I'm tempted to tell him *bed*. To touch and be touched and forget all the things we aren't to each other in favor of reaffirming everything we are.

"Want a little something to warm us up before we go back to bed?" I suggest. The snow was chilly, fake or not, and I can practically taste his mulled cider. These past few weeks he's started offering it to me at every Thursday visit. The spices he uses warm me to my toes, even once the piping hot beverage cools while we talk.

Saint nods and goes to grab a jug of cider from the fridge. I sit at his counter to watch him, admiring the way his shirt rides up to show a hint of his back. The skin just above his ass tempts me when he reaches for the tin of neatly portioned out packets of mulling spices from the top shelf. I must make some sound that reveals how much I appreciate the view. Saint glances over his shoulder to wink at me before he pulls out a pot and pours in a mix of juice and whole spices over low heat.

"Fancy," I tease him. He's the only person I know—other than my gran when I was a kid—who doesn't just use the little powder packets from the store to make his cider. His spice blend is fucking amazing. It tastes like childhood and Christmas and brings me back to a time when I believed in the impossible.

"Nothing but the best for you, babe." Saint winks at me. The endearment wallops me right in the chest. It's one he normally reserves for Carl. Everyone else is usually *darling*, or sometimes *dear*.

"Thanks," I say, mulling over how he makes me feel as the spices simmer on the stove. Saint busies himself getting out cookies from a holiday tin.

"Carl brought these over from Miss Tina's cookie swap. There's all different flavors," he explains as he offers the open tin to me. Is he nervous?

I look through the assortment and select what looks like a rum ball and a little gingerbread dinosaur iced in vibrantly colored stripes. I wiggle the dinosaur in front of me. "This is almost too cute to eat."

"Uh oh, looks like a comet is coming right for it!" Saint lifts the rum ball into the air. He holds it threateningly over the dinosaur before nudging the other cookie toward my mouth. "Run for cover, dino."

I laugh, and let myself indulge in the silliness, nibbling at the dinosaur he holds to my lips.

"That's right, go inside that perfectly safe cave, little dinosaur." Saint winks at me and I chomp on the cookie. The sweetness and warm spices are delicious. Saint's smile as he watches me indulge makes my heart beat faster. I lick my lips for any lingering traces of icing. He's staring at me so intently that there has to be a reason.

"Oh no! The comet is still coming right for that little dude." Saint holds up the second cookie for me to bite it. And I do, even though it's a little ridiculous to let the man feed me. He's such a giant goofball, but it can't cover how much he cares. I hate the idea of him cutting himself off from people out of some misplaced fear he can't be enough. It's ridiculous.

"Why don't you date?" I blurt before I can fully think it through. I can only blame being sleep-addled for that question slipping past my filters.

Saint pulls back, fingers clenching around the second bite of the rum ball. He stares resolutely over at the simmering pot. As though it suddenly requires close supervision.

"We've been over this, Angel. I'm aromantic. I don't do *falling in love*." He puts air quotes around that last bit.

"Okay. But you do love people. Carl, for one." I try not to sound accusing. Or envious of the fact he'll admit that he loves Carl, but not me. It's obvious in all the little ways he looks out for me, but I just... need something. Not more, whatever he means when he says he can't offer it. I want exactly what we have, but with a promise he won't keep pulling back the way he has been lately. Yanking the rug out from under me yet again.

"Sure. But I'm never going to be your dream boyfriend. I'm not going to suddenly start remembering or caring about our anniversaries. I'm not going to plan a date night. Or get you frivolous gifts or come home with flowers, or make you breakfast in bed with fruits cut into swans or that sort of nonsense. I'll never spontaneously bring a white Christmas to your doorstep after we have a fight or learn to sew an apology sweater."

I laugh.

"Is that what you think I want? Saint, the sweetest thing I can think of right now is someone else making me my favorite winter beverage, or heck, even remembering an offhand comment that it always reminds me of my gran. Or maybe getting to sleep in because I don't have work and someone else will actually get my kids off to school if I drop the ball. I don't want frivolous love-bombing shit from anyone. To be honest, it makes me nauseous, and I don't trust it. I just want exactly what we've been doing."

"Thursday night fuckfests with the occasional weekend sleepover and sexting to tide us over in between visits?" Saint arches an expressive brow at me. I roll my eyes at the infuriating man.

"Yeah. And I wouldn't say no to you texting that you're thinking of me while you're snuggling with Carl. Or whoever else. You keep saying we're friends, so treat me like your friend instead of freezing me out every time we get a little emotionally vulnerable because you think I might want things I never asked you for." I try not to sound as completely exasperated with him as I feel.

He was really going to push me away over that? How does he not realize by now that he's exactly what I want? I love what we have, not some idealized future version of it.

"That cuts both ways, Angel. Friends help each other without keeping score or making it into a big deal."

"It *is* a big deal when I can't pay you back."

"You don't have to!" Saint slaps his palm against the counter, smashing the remains of the cookie. I jump. The abrupt motion nearly topples my tall chair as I stand in front of it, hands braced on the counter.

I shake my head, retreating a step at the heat in his words. I can't do this. Fight. Cower in front of someone who is angry and has the power to take away so much of my happiness.

I promised myself I wouldn't be vulnerable like this again. Except, fuck, it's lonely never letting anyone in. I resist the urge to run out on this conversation.

I focus on calming my breathing. The cool granite of his countertops, the warmth of his wooden floors through my fuzzy socks, the sharp corner on his barstool bumping into my outer thigh. Breathe in his cologne and the lingering traces of spice from the cookie. The crisp bite of the cider perfuming the air as it warms. The sound of it bubbling away on the hob. And Saint's eyes on me are so full of compassion I can't tear myself away from them. I take in the stricken look on Saint's face at realizing he scared me. He wouldn't hurt me, but I don't think there's any hiding the history behind that response. So I don't try.

"I'm sorry that I raised my voice." Saint clenches his fists at his sides. He takes a deep breath. "I just wish you could accept that there aren't strings attached to anything I give you. I'm not him. Okay? I don't expect you to pay me back for every scrap of kindness."

"That isn't what I'm doing—" I stare at him as he nods impassively.

"It is, though." Saint gives me a moment to drink in that truth.

I didn't view it that way until just now. That I'm painting him with the broad brush of my past traumas. It didn't occur to me that it might hurt to be seen as a threat to my hard won freedom every time he tries to do something nice for me.

"I don't think you're the sort of person who would deliberately hurt me," I say.

Saint nods. "I'm glad, because I wouldn't. But I still keep coming up on these raw nerves of yours, and if we want to keep doing this, we need to figure out how to make that stop."

"Yeah. Same for you. I notice you pulling back, Saint. You were ready to cut and run by the end of Eliza's party. Don't think I didn't notice that."

He nods again, his usually sweet smile tinged with sorrow. "We all carry our past hurts with us, Angel. That's not unique to you. I can't tell you how often I've let my guard down with past partners, only to realize they expect me to be someone different in a relationship."

"I don't. Other than the money disparity, you are damn near perfect for me, Saint. Honestly, about the only thing I'd change if we were in an official 'relationship' is that I'd want to spend more time with you. Maybe live together some day, if you're open to that and I can get past moving in together seeming like a trap. And for you to know my kids better. Be a part of our day-to-day more."

He sucks air through his teeth. This entire conversation is fraught because there's so much hanging in the balance if it goes badly. "Want to know why I haven't?"

"You worry too much about blurry lines?" I shrug with a practiced nonchalance that is more about not scaring him off than any casual indifference to his response. It isn't hard to put together the one-to-one correlation between the times he pulls back from me and the times we really open up to each other.

"Basically, yeah." Saint shrugs. "Spending time with Owen made this all seem so much more real. I don't want to hurt your kids if I pull back again. I know that's a thing I do. It's how I protect my heart and

I couldn't stand the thought of hurting you or your kids if I let you all get any closer to me."

"So don't disappear on us." I reach over to pat his hands. "I know that's simpler said than done, but just promise to talk to us if we're asking too much from you. We can work things out as long as we talk to each other about our piles of baggage. And you know, maybe get therapy to actually work through some of it."

"Yeah." Saint snorts. "Therapy might be good. And I can promise to talk to you instead of assuming things." He cocks his head and gives me a half-smile. "You know, considering how leary both of us are at the first hint of strings, it's a miracle we let this go on long enough for me to love you."

Saint chuckles, but it's a forced sound, and he scrubs at his face, like he needs to hide from the hugeness of what he just put into words for the first time.

It floors me to hear him admit that aloud. Even couched the way he did it, my belly swoops at those words. Giddy exhilaration thrums through me, like staring down the plunge of a really good roller coaster.

"You love me?" I repeat. Letting the words sink into my soul. Letting myself hope this can be real.

"Um, yeah. Don't pretend you didn't know that." Saint crosses his arms over his chest and pouts at me. And I did know it.

I've known it from the way he takes care of me in practical ways. The times he's tucked me into his bed after I fell asleep with his mouth on me. When he made me cider and offered me and my son rides on icy roads. When he invited me to share his holiday traditions with the man he still loves in an entirely different capacity.

"I did. I didn't expect you to say it aloud." That's the truth too. And I don't need him to say it to feel his love down to the core of me. But it's really fucking nice to hear.

"Well, it's not 'in love' but I do love you, Angel. You're one of my closest friends, so I've loved you for a while now." He repeats the words that curl up inside me, just as warm and welcoming as his delicious cider. When he puts it like that—the words simple and unadorned—love doesn't scare me. How could it, when his love is in every caring gesture he makes toward me? His unprepossessing love is exactly what keeps drawing me back to him, week after week. I don't want 'in love' with all the trappings. Saint is more than enough for me.

"I love you too," I say. And because he probably needs to hear this part even more than the first part, I add, "Just the way you are."

"Yeah?" He smiles at me, so full of hope as those smile lines I love crinkle around his eyes.

"Mhm. I love the ways you show you care. I don't need flowers and sweet nothings when you're sweet enough all on your own. That isn't us. I get that Carl needs the big loud love like we saw between him and Nick earlier, and you're used to that. But over-the-top declarations and extravagant gestures make me feel like the walls are closing in. I can't handle feeling like either of us owes the other anything. There were always strings on everything with Trevor. I never knew where I stood and I always seemed to be behind on his balance sheets unless I did exactly what he wanted. I mean, I've told you what it was like toward the end. Always walking on eggshells. I can't go back to living like that."

"Never." Saint cups my cheek. "I never want to be the one to make you feel like less or like you have to compromise any part of yourself."

"I know. And if you give me enough time, I might be able to accept it even in the most jaded depths of my heart. I want the chance to build a life with you. If you can handle the fact that an irrational part of me might always worry about repeating past mistakes, no matter how different you are from him. It might take me time to trust in *myself* enough not to need an escape hatch." I can't quite meet his gaze.

Admitting this is scary when it might be too much for him, but I spent years learning not to trust my own judgment and it will take time to unlearn. We've already been doing this for over two years and it still took my kids pointing it out for me to fully realize how happy I am when I get to have time with Saint. Time to be fully myself and prioritize my own needs. I glance at his face and Saint gives me an encouraging little nod.

"That makes sense. I never want you to feel like you need an escape from me, but I always want you to have one if you ever do. It's okay if you always need to have a clear way out to feel secure. We can figure out a way to make things work. As long as you are sure you don't need the romantic stuff that I can't give you. I'm not interested in changing who I am for a lover either."

"I don't want to change you. You are exactly what I need in a partner. Dependable and there for me when I need you. We make each other smile. That's the first thing I fell for about you." I reach out to trace his laugh lines, and he leans into my reverent touch. "We can compromise on a lot, but not who we are. I want you just the way you are, Mathieu. I want us to keep making each other smile for years to come."

"Good." He beams at me as he reaches for my hands. I tangle our fingers, needing to anchor myself in his touch. "Because I want to keep loving you for as long as it takes for you to trust in us."

"Me too." I nod, a little breathless and floaty at how well this is going. Almost like the afterglow of really good sex.

"So that leaves one thing." Saint takes a deep breath, like whatever he has to say next scares him as much as promising any part of myself to a lover scares me. I hold my breath along with him. I squeeze his hand in mine, hoping I can give him the courage to take this leap into what a shared future might look like with me.

"If you'll let me, I want to love your kids too. That's why I've been pulling away the past few days. Since Owen interrogated me about our relationship, and I realized I'm already in deep with you. The idea of being in a position to break your heart is bad enough, but breaking a kid's heart is terrifying. Fuck knows I am clueless about parently duties, but you make me want to try."

"I want that too." I nod. "Maybe someday they'll see you as a father figure, if you want that. It's okay if you don't. They're old enough to form their own relationships with my partner."

"They are. And it would be an honor if they see me as their step-dad someday. As long as you are okay with it. I don't want to overstep."

"You aren't. I'd like you three to get to know each other." I let myself smile at the thought of them together.

It should be hard to give him that permission. The idea of exposing my kids to more heartbreak is scary. But I trust Saint not to put them through the same hot and cold hell of rejection they've been getting from Trevor for years. I might not trust myself to be able to make a relationship last, but Saint is too mature to take out even a messy breakup on my kids.

"You're doing fine so far. They, uh, got you a gift. For Christmas." I gesture toward where I left my bag by the door, grateful for a change of subject to steal a moment to breathe after what we just discussed.

Saint loves me and we are going to try making a future together. That doesn't feel real yet. But my kids gave their tacit blessing with that gift and I want him to be as happy about that as I am.

"They did?" Saint looks at me with a mix of interest and, well, he looks like someone who just found out his squish likes him back. Hopeful. Delighted even. "What is it?"

I laugh and turn to fetch my bag. "I don't know, but you can open it. It's Christmas now."

I wink at him and Saint follows me down his entry hall to the door, where I pull out the clumsily wrapped package and press it into his hands. "Here."

Saint grins at me with all his charm and I don't know how I got to be the one he smiles at like that, but I want to keep it. He turns the parcel in his hands and then plucks at the inexpertly applied tape until the first flap comes loose, unwrapping it with infuriating patience. I watch with bated breath, not sure what to expect.

Saint peels back the paper, still careful not to tear it, and I can tell from the backing that it's a picture frame.

"Oh." Saint glances between me and the photo, then presses it to his chest. "That Meg is sneaky."

"Yeah? Is it okay?"

"It's perfect." Saint turns the frame to show a photograph of us. It's a silly selfie he took of us in bed on one of Trevor's weekends with the kids. Nothing inappropriate. We're posed with my head resting on Saint's shoulder. His arm is wrapped around me and his lips pressed to my temple as I smiled up at the camera, utterly content in his arms. He captured it the moment before I protested that my hair was a disaster, tangled from having his fingers twined in it while we fucked the night before. At least we weren't naked under the covers, so there's nothing untoward for the kids to have seen. And my hair looks pretty good spilling across Saint's pillow.

I groan with the realization of where Meg got that picture though. Saint texted it to me. And some of the other texts in that thread were decidedly not PG.

I thought I was so clever, looking up how to lock the app and deleting any naked photos before I lent her my phone. I obviously shouldn't have been so sentimental about keeping my messages with Saint. Should have known I didn't stand a chance at outsmarting a fourteen-year-old with electronics, considering the kid has grown up with that stuff.

"We look good together, don't we?" Saint asks, looking as insecure about it as I sometimes feel.

"You always look good." I shove his shoulder, barely budging him.

"Well, so do you." Saint chuckles. He traces his fingers over the simple wooden frame carved with little scrollwork hearts. The distressed white paint matches the white sheets around Saint and me in the photo. It will look good next to his bed. The sort of thing a couple would decorate with.

"You don't have to put it on display."

"Why wouldn't I?" Saint sounds defensive as he hugs the frame tighter. Like it's precious. Like *I'm* precious.

"Might give your other dates the wrong idea?" I try to play it off as a flippant joke.

Saint smirks at me with all his usual self-assured charm. "How many other dates do you think I have?"

I shrug. That's something I pointedly don't think about, let alone ask. "As many as you want. We aren't exclusive."

"Do you want to be?" Saint offers, as if that isn't an off limits topic between us. Asking too much.

It catches me off guard, because I always assumed it wasn't an option. "Um, not if it's a deal breaker. I've already told you I have zero issues with you and Carl."

"Right, I meant, do you want sexual exclusivity? Because I thought we were dancing around the whole boyfriend conversation in the kitchen. But if that's not what you want..."

My heart beats faster, and there's an edge of nerves to it, but mostly, yes. That's what I want. "I want you to be my boyfriend in whatever way we need to define that term so it feels right for you. But only if you want that too. And I totally respect your QPR with Carl. I don't expect things with him to change on your end. Unless he'd be cool with more nights like last night?"

"I think he would be? Unless Nick smartening up changes things for us." Sadness flits across Saint's face and I know that outcome would bother him more than he's letting on. And I also know him well enough to be certain he'll accept whatever scraps of affection Carl offers him and still be the best damn friend he can. It blows me away how much I care about this man. How huge his heart is. I don't know what I'd do without all the little ways he shows his love.

"Oh, the cider! Come back to the kitchen and we can keep discussing this?" Saint suggests.

"Mm, cider." I follow Saint. He sets the photo of us on his counter, displaying it proudly before pivoting to turn off the stove. "What more is there to discuss?"

"What do I call you?" Saint asks as he ladles out the finished cider to place a steaming mug in front of me. I inhale the fragrant steam, wrapping my fingers around the warm ceramic. It's wild how something so simple can make me feel so loved. In the here and now with Saint, but also in my memories of Gran, before I grew up and realized that love can be fickle and finite.

I sip the cider. "Mm, so tasty."

"Glad you like it." Saint beams at me and takes a drink from his mug too. He sighs contentedly before turning off the stove.

I bite my lip, considering the options to answer his earlier question. We both drink more of the hot cider. Boyfriend isn't quite right. The femme options make my stomach roil; they aren't me at all. But either way, it's trying to fit into a binary box that isn't made for me. I reach for the next term that comes to mind, already knowing it isn't quite right for us either. "I suppose zucchini is already taken?"

"Yeah." He smiles, thinking of Carl. "And I mean, we aren't really platonic. How about my partner?" Saint says it like he's trying it on for size and I think I like it. "We could both go with that, if you'd like. Because if I'm going to get to know your kids now, that's a long-term commitment. It feels bigger than boyfriends. I want you to be confident that I won't flake on you or them."

That promise means more than I can say; it's yet another way he's showing he knows my heart. I nod. "That works for me."

"So, we're partners then?"

"Yeah. I like that." I lift my cider to him and we clink our mugs together.

"Partners. In that case, I'm going to put this picture of my partner and me in my room. Want to see how it looks from my bed?" He raises his eyebrow at me.

Damn that sexy smile of his still does things to me after more than a year of stolen moments in his bed. He makes my bits warm and tingly, and I want nothing more than to join him up in his room. I gulp another sip of the cider, not wanting to waste a drop of the delicious drink.

Saint reaches for the photo frame and something falls onto the counter as he picks it up.

"Oh, huh. There's a note." Saint plucks a folded square of paper from where it must have fallen out when he opened the little kickstand that holds the frame upright.

"What's it say?" I ask, all but holding my breath. My kids wrote him a note and I almost dread hearing what they have to say about my love life.

"Hmm?" Saint skims the paper, his expression inscrutable. Then, without a word, he hands it to me.

Saint,

As you can see, you make our pop happy. We both want you to keep making them happy. So, thanks for the thoughtful gifts, but all we really need from you is to keep making them smile.

Merry Christmas,

Meg and Owen

PS- Owen says he also really wants DayDreamer 2 *to go with the new console we're all pretending is a surprise, but he's a brat, so ignore him.*

PPS- Meg's a tattler, and she totally looked at all your personal messages with Pop. She says she needs brain bleach now, but you're welcome and we're all going to pretend the photo was saved to Pop's desktop.

Meg wrote most of the note, but I have to bite my lip to keep from laughing at the final postscript in Owen's less than tidy hand. They're both brats, but damn, do I love those two. I ache at not having them here to celebrate Christmas, a raw emptiness nothing can fill.

Saint does a damn good job of easing that loss, supporting me through the loneliness of missing them. It's my first Christmas with a true partner. I don't think I've ever really felt this supported and loved. I glance up from the note to see Saint smiling at me.

"Your kids are kind of awesome."

"They really are. I miss them. Distract me for a bit?"

"Sure. Come to bed with me?" Saint gathers up the framed photo in one hand and offers me the other.

"Yes, please." I take his hand and let him lead me up to his bed. It's not the first time we've stumbled down the hallway to his room because we can't keep our hands off each other. We both enjoy sex and Saint always makes it a good time.

This time is different. When I plaster myself against his back and push my hands under his shirt, there's no worry at the back of my mind that he'll shrug away from the affection. I kiss his back, between his shoulder blades. I savor his warm skin under my fingers. For once, I don't have to ignore the lurking worry that this will be the last time he lets me touch him. I run my hands up his toned abs to the firm pecs dusted in salt and pepper hair. From there, I trail my fingers to the strong shoulders that can share the weight of all my burdens.

I want to kiss the sensitive nubs of his peaked nipples, suck and nip at them until he arches into me and pins me down to fuck me. I want to tease and taunt and take. No need to hold any part of myself back from this man who has shown me time after time that he sees and accepts all of me.

Chapter 15

SAINT (DECEMBER 25TH, 2023)

HAVING ANGEL PLASTERED TO my back while their hands explore me hits differently in the light of day. Our time together is usually a fleeting thing, full of urgent kisses and frantic need. I almost never get to take my time to savor them fully, so it's gratifying to find that they're still boldly eager to be close. They still want me with a raw intensity that normally makes me head for the hills once the cum and sweat cool.

I quash that initial instinct to push them away—to focus the encounter on their pleasure while keeping them at arm's length. It's strange and wonderful to let myself just enjoy a lover's touch without overthinking how they're taking my every reaction.

I get to bask in having Angel's hands on me. No more lurking fear that they'll see through all my pretenses to the part of me that loves too hard in what so many people have told me are all the wrong ways. They're not wrong for Angel though. I'm not wrong, and it's beyond freeing to feel the truth of their earlier declarations in their every touch.

Their chest pressed to my back is nice. It's even better when I turn in the circle of their arms and join our lips in a lingering kiss as we cross the threshold into my bedroom. I fumble for my dresser to set aside the framed photo. I can position it properly later.

Angel's arms loop around the back of my neck as we kiss. They tug me down enough to get us positioned better for them to grind against my erection. And, for once, I don't have to hold back or worry that I'm sending mixed signals. There's nothing left to hide. Nothing to fear in letting myself love them with all my heart.

I slip my hands under their flowy blouse and along the lean lines of their back. Angel arches, as sweetly open to me as ever. They don't try to bite back the moan that vibrates against my lips. As we shuffle the last meter to my bed, they give in to all the ways we can give each other pleasure.

We tumble onto the duvet, still fully dressed and laughing with the sheer joy of being together. I love watching them smile and knowing that I make them happy. Our time together isn't just a respite from their burdens, but a source of actual joy that radiates from them.

We're both too eager to touch every inch of each other for either of us to separate enough to strip properly. Angel rucks my shirt up out of the way to cup my pec in one hand. Their lips mold to mine in perfect synchrony as I work their pants open enough to jerk them. They're so hard in my grasp, and I want to rub Bitsy along my length, so we can both feel how hard we make each other.

"I love you, Angel," I repeat the words that, until now, have only ever felt safe with one other person. Except as much as I love Carl, this is an expression of our closeness that Angel can share with me with an eagerness to match my own. I don't have to woo them and worry over every little gesture living up to their expectations. They are everything I never thought I could let myself have. Angel smiles that gorgeous smile, fingers tracing over my lips, like they want to savor my words.

"Mhm. Love you too. Now, get a condom and you can make love to me." Their adorable nose wrinkles. "Okay, gross, that was way too corny." We both laugh as they squirm out of my arms toward the side table. It's a relief to be able to laugh like this with them during sex. For a second there I was worried having a big relationship talk really did change things in all the ways I've spent so long fearing, but Angel is still their fun, vibrant, not at all sappy self. They snag one of the foil squares. "Suit up so you can fuck me like you love me. That sounds better."

"It does." I take the condom from them and ditch my pants so I can roll it onto my length and slick the latex with extra lube. Angel watches me reclining against my pillows with greedy longing until I arch a brow at them. "Want to climb on and ride me?"

They don't have to be asked twice, eagerly moving to straddle my hips. I have to bite my lip to hold myself back from frantically thrusting up into them while they slide down onto me. There's nothing quite like the soft give of their body accepting mine. It's so much more intense knowing they're giving me their trust and their heart, along with their body and their pleasure.

Sex with Angel has been a rush since the first time they let me bury my face between their supple thighs. It's even better knowing I never have to give up this connection. I get to keep coming with them and coming back to them, over and over. We ride the waves of pleasure together, chasing an orgasm that leaves me breathless and boneless. I'm utterly content to gaze, smitten, up at my partner as they keep fucking themself on my dick. Soon they're arching over me and don't even try to hide that it's my name they're calling as they come undone.

Angel's bare shoulders are thrown back, their hair a sex-rumpled cascade as bliss transforms their features into a perfect tableau of pleasure that I'll never tire of watching. I love being the one to make them look like that. And now I get all the time in the world to memorize every facet of their face.

Their long hair tickles me when they ease forward off my softening cock and roll into my side for post-coital kisses. I ditch the condom to deal with later, then pull them closer. It's pure luxury to let myself indulge in the sort of snuggling that we've only shared for stolen moments in the past.

Angel has been my exception to not snuggling with hookups out of expedience. We've almost always had to cut this type of intimacy short. They always have to rush back to the responsibilities that made it feel safe to keep falling for them despite all my careful walls. Now I don't have to hold back. I enfold Angel in my arms and wrap a leg over their hips, letting myself indulge in everything I've wanted and been too gun-shy to reach for. With Angel, I might just be able to have it all.

After that very enthusiastic consummation of our new relationship status, we take a cat nap tangled up together in my sheets. When we get up, Angel and I make another batch of cider, throw some store-bought cinnamon rolls in the oven, and watch Christmas movies on my couch. I can tell they miss Meg and Owen. Every time there's a kid on the screen, they fidget next to me, or snuggle in closer.

We invite Nick and Carl over for brunch, but it's basically just leftover chicken on sandwiches with a side of gooey cinnamon roll goodness. Nick and Carl don't seem to notice the slim pickings. They look as blissed out together as I feel at having Angel's place in my life firmly established.

I'm not sure how both of us being involved in new relationships is going to change things between me and Carl. The four of us sharing a meal like we've all known each other for ages goes a long way to soothing my anxieties about losing my best friend to his new relationship. Nick makes a point of being friendly with me, and that helps too. Nick and Carl stay until they have to go visit with Nick's mom at her place for their big holiday meal.

I throw a roast into the slow cooker for my Christmas dinner. It's enough to feed an entire family, but I tell myself that means I'll have leftovers. I'm not assuming Angel will stay over or bring their kids to dinner. It's a holiday. A time for family togetherness and we might not be there yet.

Angel beams when Meg texts that she and Owen are headed back from their grandmother's holiday gathering. The kids will be ready to get picked up from their dad's place in about an hour. Their smile dims when they look up from the phone to me. "I guess it's time to say goodbye?"

I nod, just as reluctant as they are for this to end. Except maybe it doesn't have to. I shake my head.

I could use the power outage at their place as an excuse. Or the fact I'm making way too much food for one. Keep some distance and pretend I'm just being a conscientious friend. But didn't we just agree to move past that maddening back and forth? I want Angel and their kids here with me today. Not all the time, not yet, but eventually.

"You can refuse if I'm overstepping, but what if you bring them here?"

Angel bites their lip and won't meet my gaze.

My heart sinks at their hesitation. "I just figured, if the power isn't back, Owen won't be able to try his new games. Plus, no power to the fridge or stove might make it hard to figure out dinner. And the heat..."

Angel narrows their eyes at me. "Are you asking because you want us here or because you pity us?"

"I want you here. The other stuff is just extra reasons."

"Okay. Good. Say that then."

"I want you here." I caress their cheek, loving that these little intimacies are enough for them. That what I have to offer, my care and love, is enough without all the fancy trappings past relationships have demanded of me. They don't need the outward proofs that don't come naturally to me.

"I don't want to push the kids into any major changes too quickly. But, yeah, Owen is going to want to play his games as soon as he opens them and I don't relish shivering in front of a dark tree. I'm just a bit sentimental about all our family ornaments."

"We could bring it all here. The gifts, the tree. Everything."

Angel gives me a look like, 'are you for real?' I have to quash the impulse to take it back, because I am absolutely for real. I want them here. Including all the family mementos that clearly hold meaning for them. And if I'm really lucky, someday I might have some part of those memories twined through my life too. One day, if I play my cards right, all those treasured ornaments will adorn our shared tree each year. But that's skipping ahead, and this is about meeting Angel and their kids where they are comfortable rather than trying to take over Christmas.

"So, we're just going to grinch all the Christmas cheer from my place and bring it back here?"

I snort and try to look seductive as I say, "I wouldn't put it quite like that. But if you want me to paint my face green and put on a Santa suit for some roleplay, I'm game."

Angel kisses me through their laughter. "I don't think your heart could grow any bigger, you menace. If we're going to bring Christmas here and pick up the kids on time, we should get going though."

"On it." I head for the door, Angel right behind me. We take their truck, since they argue that there's a lot to move and they don't want the boxes to damage my car. I don't really care about scuffed seats or tracked snow, but I'm not about to say that when they're clearly daunted by any display of my finances. So we take the truck back to their place.

The power is on. Which means they probably won't have to throw out the food from the fridge. I hope. Angel shrugs that off when I mention it, though I notice the tightness around their lips.

I follow them to the tree and pull up short at the familiar ornament, front and center, right at eye level. My gnome with the rainbow hat. It could be a coincidence, but it's hanging there among the baby hand-prints and pride flags. It feels like a piece of me is there next to everything else that's important to Angel. Like the Christmas angel ornament clashing with the decor on my tree at home, because it reminds me of them. My heart beats harder in my chest as I reach out to poke the gnome's fluffy beard.

"It reminds me of you." Angel reaches past me to remove it and sets it in a box of things to bring with us to my place. I turn to capture their lips in a kiss. Angel moans against my mouth, but reluctantly pulls away before I can move to deepen it. "Stop that; we don't have much time before I need to get the kids."

"Right. I'll start bringing presents out to the car while you pick what else to take with us. Is there anything we should leave here?"

"No, it can all come." Angel moves around the tree, plucking their favorite memories from the branches. I'm still glowing with the warmth of making that cut with my gnome.

"Next year we'll have to get aro and ace flags to represent you and Carl," Angel observes as they arrange the bi and trans ornaments in their box.

My grin makes my cheeks ache. The tacit acknowledgement that Carl is my family, ex or not, eases a tension I didn't realize I was carrying deep in my chest.

Angel could have offered to just get an aro flag, but the ace one encompasses both of us and I love that my partner made a point to include him too. Angel understands me in ways I never really let myself believe were possible before them. Is it any wonder I love them to pieces?

I finish loading presents into the truck while Angel packs up the last few decorations they want to bring with us. It's mostly ornaments from the tree. We just have time to go back to my place and set everything up for the kids before Angel needs to leave for Trevor's place.

Once again, I carry the presents while Angel sets to work, adding their memories to my tree. Once everything is inside, I hand them ornaments as they add them amongst the sparkling generic silver and gold baubles I got on discount after Carl and I split up.

It took me a few years to get a tree after our divorce. These ornaments look classy and modern and they utterly lack the heart and soul Carl puts into the tree we shared while we were together. That made it easier to bear the chasm of loneliness the holidays always brought with them. The ache for a future we couldn't reconcile.

This year feels different with every ornament Angel adds to my tree. It's like they're breathing life back into a holiday that used to make me ache for everything I'm not. Not because I want to change, but because it's always seemed inevitable that the people I start to let in want me to be someone else. Or they move on past the point where my ways of loving them can fulfill their needs.

Carl has always been the exception to that. But our routines are going to change if he and Nick work out the way I hope they do. Not necessarily for the worse, but change is still hard. It's a thrill to have this new partnership with Angel to explore.

"There, what do you think?" Angel asks when they finish by placing my gnome next to the angel. They shoot me a questioning glance as they step back beside me to take in their work.

"It's perfect." A chaotic fusion of my staid decor with all the vibrancy of Angel and their kids. Like an artistic representation of the fact that Angel has been breathing life into my boring beige routines for years now. A bright spot in my days.

I sling my arm around them and kiss along their neck. Angel giggles and squirms in my arms, wriggling closer to me and making me wish we had all the time in the world to be together like this.

Their phone rings and we both sober as they answer it.

"Yeah, I'll be there to get them as soon as I can. Give me about five minutes," Angel says.

I don't catch Trevor's reply, but Angel winces and mouths a curse.

"No, I'm not at home." Angel grits their teeth and I rub a soothing circle on their back. I wish I could take away the stress. Or wave a wand to make Trevor nicer to them, but all I can really do is support them.

"None of your business. Just have them ready, please?"

Angel holds the phone away from their ear, and I catch some angry insults. It's so tempting to butt in. Threaten him with legal action. Tell him exactly what I could do to him if Angel gave me permission to go on the offensive for all the ways he's broken the terms of their divorce decree. But Angel doesn't want me to be their fixer. They just want my support. So I hold them and comfort them and bite my tongue about the verbal abuse spewing from their phone. For now.

"Okay. Be there soon. Bye." Angel hangs up with a weary sigh. "Fuck."

"Yeah."

"If he wasn't leaving the province in a week, I'd be sorely tempted to take you up on your offer to take him back to court." They force a dry chuckle as they knuckle at their eyes.

"I'd love nothing more than to go after him to the full extent of the law." I kiss their temple. "It would be sketchy as fuck to represent you now that you're my partner. But I'd consider it for you."

Angel slumps in my arms. "I appreciate the thought. It's fine though. I have it in writing that he doesn't want to deal with visitation anymore."

That trips all my warnings. "Yeah, you are going to need him to sign an updated visitation agreement. To be on the safe side."

"I do? There's only a week before he's gone."

"I'll draw something up for you tomorrow. Hopefully, he'll sign it without any fuss. I can draft a letter that makes it clear signing is in his best interest if he doesn't want to complicate his move."

"Yeah?"

"Yeah."

"I don't want the kids to ever question whether we had any sway over this. It's going to be hard enough when they realize he's not coming back. I don't want them to think for a second that I made him give up his rights or had any role in him leaving."

"They're smart. I think they know where they stand with both of you, my dear. That's not a betrayal you're capable of. It's going to be alright. But you need to cover your ass. The kids need to stay here. Where they are loved and wanted, not end up dragged off to another province where they don't know anyone as part of some twisted power play."

"Yeah. You're right. Are you sure you don't mind drawing up the papers?"

"No. I help my friends where I can." It's a relief that Angel realizes being grouped among my friends isn't a slight against how important they are to me. I can tell them that and they just give me a grateful smile.

"Thank you, Saint."

"Anytime, Angel." I seal that with a kiss, then I point them toward the door and pat their butt. "The sooner you get the kids, the sooner we can celebrate Christmas with them. Go. Don't let him take another minute of your joy, okay?"

"Yeah. Be back soon." They flash me a tight smile.

"You can bring the Mercedes if you want. Owen would love that."

Angel snorts. "Tempting, but I don't want to rile Trevor up more than I already have. Next time?"

"Next time," I agree.

I watch them drive off. Then I busy myself making sure everything is perfect for the kids' arrival. I rearrange the presents under the tree, including one I got for Angel. Among all the parcels, there's another gift for me. It fits in my palm and I'm tempted to peek under the paper. I recognize Owen's messy scrawl from the sweet note the kids wrote me with their other gift.

One little peek won't hurt. Except, when I give in to the impulse, the crudely handmade aro pride ornament hits me like a gut punch. It's a regular Christmas ball painted with wide dark green, light green, white, gray, and black stripes from top to bottom. Angel told me more about what the flags mean to them while we were decorating. That it's their family's way of affirming their love for each other. I think back to my chat in the car with Owen. How I came out to the kid without really meaning to. And this is another sign he's ready to embrace me as a part of his family. I'm going to do everything in my power to make sure he never regrets that.

Sure, it's terrifying to think those two kids might come to rely on me. I don't know how Angel has done it alone these past years, but I'm going to be the best damn step-dad I can be for them. They're worth it. Angel is worth it.

Chapter 16

ANGEL (DECEMBER 25TH, 2023)

I'M ON TENTERHOOKS AS I approach Trevor's front door for what might well be the last time. That's a strange realization. This place that's been a part of my kids' routine for years isn't going to be a part of their lives anymore after this week.

Trevor and I agreed to tell them about his move after the holidays. I even offered him one last overnight since the kids are on break for the entire week. Owen will need a chance for some closure. Meg will realize what her father's big move means and just be pissed off at him, but she deserves a chance to tell him that to his face.

I have appointments scheduled for both kids with their old family therapist for early next month. The situation with Trevor sucks, but we'll get through this together. Another reason to take things slowly with Saint instead of rushing into more upheaval in my kids' lives.

That's an excuse though. Having another supportive adult around can only be a positive development. And I deserve to be happy too. Saint has been such a bright spot for me lately. Or at least, he is when he's not backing away—and I am fairly confident that he won't be doing that anymore after our conversation earlier.

It's okay to bring the kids back to his place with me tonight. They've both picked up on how much time I spend with Saint. Neither of them seems upset about it. I'm being ridiculous as I linger on Trevor's front steps, putting off the inevitable, wavering over my decisions.

Trevor has a way of making me second-guess everything. I thought that would end when I left him, but it's still hard to trust my own judgment some days. Much as the news of his move is going to hurt the kids, a part of me is selfishly relieved it will mean less contact.

Meg opens the door before I can knock and storms down the steps, her overstuffed bag bumping down the steps behind her. She packed light in anticipation of holiday gifts, and from the way her bag bulges now, it looks like her grandmother didn't disappoint.

"He's not coming back, is he?" Meg asks me.

My heart sinks. Trevor told them about the move ahead of schedule. Of course he did. It was foolish to believe he wouldn't take the chance to ruin the rest of Christmas for me. Ugh.

Sometimes I feel like I'm paranoid about him, and then he does shit like this and I'm not crazy for thinking he does it on purpose. I'm not.

"No. He told me he isn't," I admit. I open my arms to her. Meg stares at me, trembling with anger for a long time before she caves and crashes down the steps and into my arms. She leaves her heavy bag on the stairs.

"I hate him," Meg growls through tears as I rock her in my arms. "I hate him so much."

"That's alright." I don't contradict her. She's allowed to be angry. As helpless as I feel to help her through this, I can at least give her a safe space to work through her emotions about it. Even if a part of her hates me too. She eventually pulls away to scrub at her tear-bright eyes.

"Owen is excited to visit Calgary. Dad said they'll check out the Stampede this summer."

I purse my lips.

Meg slumps. "It's not happening, huh?"

I shake my head minutely. "I'm sorry."

Meg huffs. "He's an asshole. Why don't you ever call him out?"

"Because he's your father, and as much as he infuriates me, you kids love him."

"I don't." Meg shakes her head vehemently. But there's a part of her that does. She wouldn't be so mad if she wasn't hurt and betrayed right now. I don't call her out on the lie. She probably doesn't fully realize it is one.

"Owen does," I counter instead, desperately clinging to my calm.

The fight goes out of Meg. "Yeah, well, he doesn't deserve Owen." She stoops to pick up her bag. "I'll be in the truck. Owen's almost ready."

I watch Meg stomp down the slushy path and heft her bag into the back of my vehicle. Once she's buckled into the passenger seat, I go to knock on Trevor's door. With any luck, this is the last time I'll have to stand in front of him, like a supplicant at his mercy.

"Just a sec!" Owen calls, his voice muffled through the door.

A moment later, the door flies open and I can see that my son has been crying. He dashes at his red-rimmed eyes. My heart aches for him, I wish all over again that I could take away his pain, do something to make this all better the way I used to be able to kiss away his boo-boos. I reach for him, patting his shoulder, to reassure us both that I'm here for him.

Owen sniffles. "Hey, Pop. I just need to grab some stuff from my room."

"Sure. Is your dad here?" Not that I want to see Trevor, but Owen's comment reminds me I probably need to make arrangements for any stuff they've left here.

"I'm right here," Trevor barks as he stomps toward me. Owen scurries down the hallway to his room. Trevor has the decency to wait until our son's door closes to tear into me. "I don't appreciate you being fuck knows where when you're supposed to be picking up the kids."

"Where I spend my time is none of your business, Trevor." I try to keep my cool. "Do the kids have anything here that I need to pick up before you move? Or did you want to leave their stuff with your mom?"

"I'll give it to Mom for when they visit her."

"Sure. Did you still want to take them one night this week since you already told them about the move?"

"I'm a little busy getting everything packed, Angie," he drawls his stupid nickname for me like he's doing me a favor. "You can figure out your own childcare for the school break."

"Right. I'll do that." I have to bite my cheek to keep my cool with him. My fists clench so tight my nails dig painfully into my palms. I count down from ten twice. "Well, I'll just take Owen's bag and let you say your goodbyes. When he's ready, I'll be out front waiting."

I don't wait for a reply, just bend to snag the strap of Owen's duffel bag, and haul it up to my shoulder. I can credit T with making the lift easier than it was even a few years ago. Now I can heft the kids' heaviest gear with impunity. Although Owen is still approaching the limits of my ability to carry him these days.

I shut the door, but I linger on Trevor's front steps, waiting for Owen. I'm not trying to eavesdrop or anything, but I have an ear out for any sign my son might need me to intervene—raised voices or anything. Whatever I'm expecting doesn't happen. Meg texts to ask what the holdup is. I tell her to be patient and watch through the window as she slumps dramatically in the passenger seat, curled over her phone.

A few long moments later, Owen slips out through the front door. He's clutching his ratty old baby blanket to his chest. It was a lumpy and misshapen thing when his grandmother and I first knit and pieced together the granny squares in every shade of blue we could find. That blanket and the even messier pink one we made for Meg are my only attempts at knitting.

In my defense, I was not at my best, hormonal and pregnant and miserable from living in Trevor's mom's basement. I missed my gran. When I told my ex-mother-in-law about how Gran made similar blankets for me and my brother when we were born, she offered to help me carry on the tradition for my kids.

My own mother wouldn't even talk to me, and here was Trevor's mom, keeping my family traditions alive. Despite having as little crafting experience as I did, she helped me. I don't know how her son ended up so callous, but I will always make sure the kids have a relationship with his mother. No matter how Trevor behaves or how many tantrums he's thrown over the years about me still spending time with his mom.

Owen brought the blanket over here ages ago, when he said he couldn't sleep at Trevor's. I told him since Grandma helped me make it, that it's like he's wrapping our love around himself when he snuggles under it.

My heart squeezes uncomfortably tight against my ribs at that visceral reminder that Owen is losing something important tonight. This isn't his home anymore. And somehow the man inside can let our son—both of our children—walk away without a fight. That crushes me, too close to my own deeply buried wounds.

It's not the same thing, not quite, but it still guts me. I wish I could wrap both of my children up in my love and shield them from this pain. Since I can't, I do the next best thing. I drape my arm around Owen's narrow shoulders to guide him to the truck. I help him stow his things in the bed and make sure he buckles into the back bench seat.

Then I pull back onto the icy road, away from Trevor's place. The kids are subdued as we drive, but I can't put off telling them where we're going for long. Even if it might open a can of worms that I'm not ready to handle. I don't expect them to bounce right back from Trevor's news—I should have expected him to wield it like a weapon, but the timing hurts.

I ask about their holiday so far and get noncommittal one-word replies. The food was good. Their cousins are fine. Grandma says *hi* to me. They're a bit more animated when they tell me about their gifts. Owen got a cool custom display rack for his old tae kwon do belts. His uncle promised to drop it off next week, since Trevor didn't have room for it in the car. Meg got a makeup kit that she's been eyeing for her dance shows, and then they lapse back into silence.

Their quiet brooding makes me question whether it's the right time to share what Saint and I discussed about our relationship. I don't know if now is the right time to spring a new partner on them, even if they sort of already know. But I can't exactly hide the fact our cozy family Christmas is waiting for us at his place.

"We lost power last night, so Saint invited us to have our Christmas at his house," I explain as I turn toward his place instead of home. "Is that alright?"

"Yeah, Saint is pretty cool," Owen says. "He got my class brownies and grapes."

"Did he? When was that?"

"Friday, on the way to school. I, uh, forgot to give you the sign-up sheet for our class party."

He didn't forget, he just knew it would be a strain on our budget. I quash my immediate reaction of wanting to pay Saint back for the snacks. I bite back an apology for the inconvenience and for not being able to give my kid the entire world on my own.

"Oh, I'm glad you remembered in time for the party. Did you thank Saint?" I leave the little lie unchallenged.

"Obviously, yes. Did you give him our present?" Owen asks, bouncing in his seat with a hint of his usual bubbly energy returning.

"I did."

"And?" Meg prompts, trying to maintain her teenage aloofness even though I can tell she cares about Saint's reaction to their gift. In my periphery, I can even see she's looking at me instead of her phone.

"He loved it." I smile for the kids and they smile back tightly. It's clear on their faces that they're still hurting, but that's to be expected, given the circumstances.

I should tell them where things stand with Saint. They clearly have an inkling of who he is to me, and what I want with Saint will mean changes for them; they deserve to be kept in the loop about my life choices. It's just hard to put into words. When it was just me and Saint in the safe little self-care bubble of his home, it didn't seem so scary to think of a future with him in it. Laying that hope bare for my children is terrifying. And Trevor's timing is garbage.

It's a lot for me, and I'm an adult. I'm gripping the steering wheel too tight. Am I making the right call by bringing my kids to my new partner's house right after they got dumped by their father? I hope so.

"Good." Meg smiles, looking self-satisfied as she turns back to her phone.

"I knew he'd like it," Owen pipes up. "I picked the frame."

"You did good. It's a great picture." I force myself to relax. Both kids seem fine with the plan to spend our holiday evening with Saint. I can bring up privacy and Meg snooping through my messages to get that photo another time. At least I deleted our more explicit photo exchanges before handing over my phone to her.

"Because you're happy," Meg says like it's obvious and I'm being a ridiculous old fogey for not realizing that on my own. She might be right.

"So, what would you say if I told you that Saint and I are in a relationship?"

"Good for you. I'm not calling him Dad," Meg says.

"You don't have to call him anything you aren't comfortable with," I assure her.

"But Saint said he doesn't date," Owen says, sounding puzzled.

"That's true, but we both enjoy spending time together and we agreed that we want more time with each other. And he wants to get to know you kids, because you're the most important people in my life."

"Cool. If he's going to be our new step-dad, do you think he'll let me drive his car?" Owen bats his pretty eyes at me and I have to bite my cheek to keep from laughing.

"You aren't driving anything anytime soon, kiddo." I don't address the step-dad comment because I'm not ready to go there yet, but it wouldn't be the worst outcome by any means. I hope Saint agrees with that.

Owen sighs dramatically. "Ugh, fine. Can I at least ask him to drop me off in it again? Mikey was super impressed on Friday."

"I'm sure that can be arranged." I try to hide my amusement at his priorities. And it's strange to accept that my kid might ask my partner for a ride so casually, but isn't that what I'm signing up for? Moving toward sharing our lives and responsibilities?

It's still sinking in that Saint wants me—and my kids—in his life. Enough to make us all welcome in his home tonight. It's just on the edge of too much. The scared and scarred parts of me can't help seeing all the loveliness of him inviting us into his home as gilded cage bars. A trap that might ensnare me in another situation I can't escape.

Except I can have a way out this time, my teaching certification and Gran's inheritance, if I accept Marcus's generosity. Besides, we discussed this and Saint isn't the sort to lock me away or force me into a form he prefers. He's always been more likely to stand back and admire my spread wings rather than attempt to clip them like so many before him. My parents and Trevor chiefly, but others too.

Every nosy bystander who makes it seem like I have to pick a side—masc or femme, girl or boy—to be safe in public. Rather than existing in the liminal in-between that feels the most like myself. The customers who made it easier to earn a living with a low-cut blouse emphasizing the curves that made my skin crawl and a flirty smile. It's different working for tips these days, with my flat chest and the patchy wisps of facial hair. My beard is only now starting to fill in if I forget to shave for a few days after years of taking low-dose testosterone.

When I'm with Saint, I'm safe to be myself. I just hope that someday my kids can feel as safe and comforted by his steady caring as I do. Even if I sometimes doubt everything about myself and my judgment, I have no doubts that Saint will never let them down like Trevor has. Saint won't take back his heart once he's given it. His dependability is one thing I love about him. It's why I trust him enough to let him into my kids' lives.

THE KIDS QUIETLY TAKE in all the nice decorative touches as I let us inside Saint's place. He didn't lock up behind me earlier since I was coming right back. It's strange to see the familiar entryway where I've given Saint so many breathless kisses through their eyes. It's tidier than our place, with all the kids' winter and school stuff piled on rickety old shelves and mismatched plastic hooks. He's got fancy art on the walls. Pictures that aren't family photos and crayon drawings.

From the muffled kitchen noises and smells, Saint has a pot of cider simmering on his stove. The entire house is warm and so inviting that it's tempting to imagine making a home here as I watch my kids in my partner's space for the first time.

The air is redolent with holiday spices and the savory aroma of the roast Saint put in his slow cooker this morning. Did he intend to feed my family when he did that? The meal I can smell simmering means something. Saint wants my kids to feel like the family we talked about trying to be to each other. It's a tangible way of living up to a promise so lofty it's all but impossible to believe in the abstract.

We're all quiet with our thoughts as we remove our outerwear in his entryway. Meg places her boots neatly beside mine. Owen kicks his shoes off willy-nilly, and I have to remind him to tidy them next to ours.

"Buddy, we're guests," I remind him, gesturing at the offending footwear. It's a reminder to myself too. This isn't home and Saint might be my partner, but this is still new and tentative.

"Sure, Pop." Owen reluctantly lines his boots up next to his sister's, chin jutting out petulantly.

Right. Probably not the best thing to remind him of during our family time, after he just got relegated to feeling like less than a guest in his father's home. But it's true. Much as I want to build some kind of future with Saint, we're his guests tonight.

Lucky for me, Saint swoops in to defuse the moment.

"Angel?" Saint pokes his head around the corner from the open kitchen area. He flashes his million-watt smile and my heart melts. This might not be home yet, but someday I could picture coming home to him and his smile and our family photos joining his austere art pieces on the walls. "I'm glad you're back. Come on in and make yourselves at home. I was just thinking I'd reheat some of the cinnamon rolls from breakfast for the kids while we wait for dinner to finish cooking. Do you two prefer them frosted or plain?"

"Frosted, please," Owen says, drawn toward the heavenly smells, despite what must have been a huge holiday feast at his grandmother's house earlier. He's definitely got a growth spurt coming.

"Iced." Meg nods. She perks up too, following her brother down the hall. I bring up the rear and soon the four of us are congregating in Saint's kitchen. Hard to believe I partook in a family brunch with Saint, Carl, and Nick right here just a few hours ago. The juxtaposition of my kids and me sharing our family dinner with Saint in the same seats where I joined my partner's family tradition with Carl earlier almost sends me reeling again.

The kids and Saint exchange greetings. He asks them about dinner with their grandmother and cousins. I let their answers roll over me as if I wasn't once a part of that family too. As if they didn't just lose their strongest connection to it.

It's a lot. And I can't rush this. Not when the kids already have so much else going on. It all seems impossibly tangled. I just want Saint to hold me together because a part of me wants to run right back out his door rather than risk another heartbreak for my babies. Or myself.

While I'm struggling to control my emotions, Saint oohs and aahs over my kids' descriptions of the gifts they got from their extended family. He ladles out four steaming mugs of mulled cider and sets two perfectly iced cinnamon rolls in front of my kids. Then he comes around the table and hugs me from behind, tipping my face toward him for a quick kiss.

"Hey, you with us, Angel?" Saint asks, giving my shoulder a squeeze.

"Hm? Yeah." I force a smile past my worries.

"Owen asked if we have to wait until we go home to open presents," Meg says, as if I should have heard the question the first time. I should have, but my thoughts are scattered and I'm having a hard time believing I can really have this; my kids sitting here smiling and talking to the man who makes me feel like I don't have to carry the entire world on my shoulders all alone.

"Want to do presents now? The roast should be ready by the time we finish," Saint offers, his hand still on my shoulder, steadying me.

"Let's do presents." I nod. "We brought everything over here because I figured you've been more than patient waiting to open yours, Owen."

"I have. I definitely made the nice list." He nods earnestly, already standing as he shoves the last bite of his cinnamon bun into his mouth. Owen eyes the outer crust of Meg's that she left on her plate.

"Go for it, you bottomless pit." Meg nudges her plate toward her brother. He gobbles down the last bite of her treat while she rolls her eyes and smiles affectionately at him.

I love watching them together. The two of them share a bond I'm only now starting to really form with Marcus. My big brother rarely had time for me. I was forever following him around as a kid. Desperate to connect with him in a home where some part of me always felt like an outsider. I am so proud of my kids and their close friendship.

"Presents?" Owen turns to me with his cheeks stuffed full of sweets like a chipmunk.

"Chew your food." I bite back a laugh at how adorable my kid is as he carefully finishes what's in his mouth as fast as he can. "Everything is under the tree. You can open the first one, since Meg got to open her big present early."

I point toward the glowing tree in Saint's living room. Its monochrome gold and white elegance is now broken up with our family memories. That's almost enough to make this feel like we've found our way home. Almost.

"Score!" Owen fist pumps as he scurries over to the tree to check out his present haul. Meg follows at a more sedate—if no less eager—pace. Saint tugs me in against his side as we follow the kids to the tree. With the hasty decor we added from my place, Saint's tree looks like it could be a fusion of our lives, and somehow, it just all works.

Watching the kids open and exclaim over the gifts that Saint bought for them, it's like I've stepped forward in time to that dreamy future full of possibilities. A shared home that's full of family and love. A partner by my side who adores my children as much as I do. Who supports me when I need to lean on him. I squeeze his hand and Saint gives me a nervous smile. He nuzzles into my neck.

"How am I doing?" Saint asks.

I snort, and then I realize he seriously needs me to reassure him for once. It's amazing to be there for him, it helps me understand the fulfillment he claims to get from being there for me all the time. I kiss his cheek and squeeze his hand. "You're doing perfect. They like you. Just keep being yourself."

"Here, Pop, we got you something." Meg thrusts a little gift bag into my hands. I pull out an apple shaped ornament that reads *World's Best Teacher* in a chalky scrawl across a little slate rectangle tag. "Owen and I just wanted you to know that we're proud of you and you're going to be awesome in the classroom after break. Even though I'd probably die of embarrassment if you were teaching my classes. So thanks for getting assigned to the second graders." My daughter winks at me.

I tear up, bursting with pride and joy and just everything. It's overwhelming to hear that sort of praise, a glimmer of a future adult relationship with my kids where they start to see me as a whole person instead of just their parent. I want that, it's a hollow ache for something I never got that I can give them. I want to have a lifelong relationship with my daughter where we are both proud of each other, because I am just bursting with pride for her and Owen. So much of what I do is about giving Meg and Owen the best in life, and this gift, acknowledging my accomplishments outside of them, feels incredible.

I hug both kids and add the apple to the tree with the other important milestone ornaments.

Owen has a ceramic tae kwon do shoe to commemorate his first competition last year. Meg has a ballerina from when she earned her laces. The pirate flag. My lion from going on T. A story of our greatest hits. I get a little choked up looking at it here in Saint's home and imagining all our future milestones together, joining the rest among the branches. Someday his aro flag will hang next to my trans pride ornament. I want that.

Saint grins as he wades into the torn paper to help the kids distribute the remaining gifts. The kids laugh and stick bows to him. We end up tossing balled up wrapping paper at each other in an all out giggling indoor version of a snowball fight.

I didn't think Owen and Meg could be this happy today after the news Trevor gave them. I'm under no illusions that it's going to be simple adjusting to that change, but something about Saint makes it easy to believe that everything will work out fine. Somehow, he helped me give the kids a Christmas to remember for all the right reasons when today could have ended in tears. And I know I made the right call bringing them here tonight, sharing the three most important people in my life with each other.

Owen grabs the last two presents, both of them lumpy and patched together with too much tape to cover irregular shapes underneath. He hands one to me and one to Saint.

"What's this?" Saint asks, but there's a strange gleam in his eyes, like he knows. I'm clueless as I poke at the shape under the paper. "You already gave me a present, bud."

Owen shrugs and scuffs his toe against the carpet, not quite looking at either of us. "Yeah, well, this one is special."

"Who should go first?" Saint asks.

"Pop." Owen says.

Meg reaches up from her spot on the floor amongst the discarded wads of paper and squeezes her brother's hand. They're so damn sweet together. I'm not sure why she thinks he needs the support, but I carefully peel the wrappings from a rainbow striped, felted parrot ornament. The bird is wearing an eye patch and a pirate hat at a jaunty angle. It's as cheery and colorful as the kid offering it to me.

I glance between the flag and my kiddo. "Yeah? Is this to upgrade your pirate flag?"

He nods, ducking his head bashfully. "I ordered it from Miss Tina at the market. So..." He shrugs and gestures at the rainbow ornament, then shoots up some jazz hands. "Surprise? I'm pretty sure I'm gay."

"Cool, thanks for letting me know. I love you, kiddo." I stand and pull him into a hug, not surprised in the least. It's still beyond gratifying to hear him say the words. For him to know himself and be comfortable sharing with me, I must be doing something right with this parenting thing. Instead of barraging him with questions that he might not want to answer—especially in front of Meg and Saint—I bite my lip. "No matter what."

"I know, Pop. That's why I told you." Owen sighs, rolls his shoulders and turns to face Saint. "Did Pop tell you about the ornaments?"

"That they're a coming out tradition for your family?" Saint asks, gesturing toward the tree.

I'm pretty sure I know what's in Saint's present now. And I can't help tensing at the message the kids are sending with that gift. They're inviting him into my favorite of our traditions. One that I hope lets them know they are safe, loved, and accepted all year round. For every part of themselves that they chose to share with me and for all the parts they aren't ready to share yet. They are inviting him into our family every bit as much as I did by agreeing to have our Christmas with him tonight. And they got that gift for him before Saint and I even made things official.

"Yeah. Sort of. They mean that you're family for keeps." Owen sums it up perfectly. "So, since you know, you can open that one now. It was my idea, because of what we talked about in your kick-ass car, but Meg agreed that we should give it to you. Mikey's mom helped me to paint it before their party on Friday."

Saint hesitates, and I hope the reality of my kids seeing him as family doesn't scare him away. It did at Eliza's party not two days ago. But we discussed his reservations, and he said he's okay with this. Fuck, I hope this doesn't make it too real and scare him away. His eyes are wide and bright as he gives me a beseeching look over the present. My heart is pounding so hard it seems like it might burst right out of my chest if he reacts poorly to my kids' gesture.

"Go on, open it," I say, trying to keep things light, even as my heart is in my throat waiting for his reaction to this emotional escalation. We discussed that I won't ask for more than he has to give, but is this too much for him?

"One of us," Meg chants slowly.

"One of us!" Owen takes up the words. The two of them repeat it three more times before Saint chuckles as he slits open the tape. He withdraws an aro flag ornament that makes my breath catch in my throat.

"Guess this makes me officially one of you?" He holds it up with a grin that makes all the laugh lines I love around his eyes crinkle. Fuck, I love him.

"Come on, let's put both of these on the tree and make it officially official. Shall we, Owen?" Saint gestures.

I hand Owen the rainbow parrot so the two of them can hang their ornaments next to the ones that are already there. The array of pride flags, handprints, and every other important moment memorialized amongst the lights. Meg grins at me as we watch Owen and Saint adjust the placement of the final two ornaments and then turn to face us just as the kitchen timer trills.

"Perfect timing." Saint grins. "Who's ready to eat?"

"I'm starving!" Owen turns toward the kitchen.

"I could eat. Dinner smells pretty good," Meg agrees, following her brother into Saint's kitchen.

Saint hangs back to wrap an arm around me and steal a kiss next to the tree. "So, guess they're keeping me?"

"Yes. We're all keeping you." I loop my arms around Saint's neck and indulge in one more lingering Christmas kiss.

He makes my knees weak. I cling to the man I've been falling in love with more every Thursday for years until the kids call for us to feed them. The very ordinariness of that feels miraculous, and I am going to enjoy every ordinary second the four of us have together.

We sit around Saint's table together after helping him set it with the food he prepared. It could be awkward, but Owen breaks the tension by singing about the potatoes. That gets Saint laughing and singing along as we all fix our plates. Meg rolls her eyes at their antics, but she can't quite hide her smile.

Saint's eyes meet mine as he sings into his spoon. He rocks out with Owen like he's not new to the whole 'nurturing young minds' gig, and I swear my heart might just explode at how sweet he is with my kids. Watching them together, I'm certain this is going to work.

As we're eating, Owen asks if he can have a ride in Saint's car later. Which somehow segues into Meg grilling Saint about his job and what he actually does all day. And before my eyes, my kids are getting to know the other most important person in my life. It makes me so damn grateful and proud of them. They could have let Trevor derail the rest of our day, instead we enjoy a delicious meal.

After the food and a quick video chat with Marcus for our families to wish each other a merry Christmas, Owen demands to watch Rudolph for his annual sing-along. Saint volunteers to help him gather snacks while Meg goes to see what Saint has for streaming services. She gets the show cued up.

Saint and Owen's snack expedition turns up two tins of cookies, what little Saint still has of Gran's fudge that I gave him, and a bag of popcorn. Saint texts Carl an invite for him and Nick to join us after their visit with Nick's mom. We don't wait for them to start the movie though.

Saint's sectional is huge, but the four of us clump cozily together in the middle. We snuggle to watch the movie under a festive red and green throw blanket that looks like it migrated over here from Carl's place. It's perfect, giving my kids a Christmas surrounded by family and love.

Epilogue

ANGEL (DECEMBER 25TH, 2026)

MEG AND OWEN HANG up from their biannual video chat with Trevor after about five minutes. It's not ideal, but that's about all the parenting he can handle and the kids seem to have accepted that once they got past the initial grief and anger. Moving past the hurts he left us with is still a work in progress, for me as much as the kids, but I've been learning to lean on our support network more.

It was only a few months after Trevor left that Meg stopped trying to call him. Owen took a little longer to stop expecting the phone—which I got him so he could call his dad—to ring. That was when I caved and accepted Gran's money from Marcus. Because my practicum meant long hours and fewer shifts at the diner and something had to give, so it was either that or accept Saint's financial help. I took the family money.

There was more than I expected in the account from Gran's estate. Enough to let me feel secure that I would always have a way out if things ever stop working with Saint. Enough that when he asked us to move in last year, the kids and I accepted. I'd just gotten hired full time as a teacher with some online tutoring on the side to bring in extra cash, the timing was right for us.

Meg rolls her eyes and throws herself dramatically onto the couch between Saint and me. The kids still call him Saint most of the time, but they tell everyone he's their step-dad. Owen says it's because having a Saint who loves them means more than an empty title ever could.

"Ugh, now that's over with, can we open presents?" Meg complains, but I can see the underlying hurt. Trevor's abandonment still takes a toll on both kids in different ways. Meg's mostly past being angry at him. Owen is quiet, his hurt clear. If the past is any guide, he'll be mostly over it by the time we finish opening presents. I tug my gangly teenager down onto the couch on my other side and hug him, ruffling his scruffy hair and tickling his ribs.

"I don't know. Are you ready for presents too, Owen?"

Owen tries to resist for a second, fighting to keep his face impassive before writhing next to me. "Okay, I give!"

I stop tickling him and tug him down to brush a kiss to his temple. I'm still getting used to his new height. Kid shot up like a weed over the summer, like he took having his thirteenth birthday on the horizon as permission to be taller than me. The brat.

"Pop!" Owen groans, but he's fighting a smile.

"Love you, kid."

"Yeah. I know." He cracks a smile and snuggles into my side. As much as a teenager is willing to snuggle with his parent. He stoops to rest his head on my shoulder.

"Presents?" Meg reminds us.

"Yeah, Pop, presents?" Saint reaches over Meg to tug on my free shoulder.

Meg sticks her tongue out at him. "What? I'm allowed to be excited."

"It's almost like you think you're on Santa's nice list." Saint winks at her.

Meg pouts. "I'm always nice."

"More like Saint's nice list," Owen interjects, since he knows which of us is the sucker to give his holiday wishlist to.

"Sure, kid," Saint teases as he stands up to approach the tree. It's covered in memories of the life we're building together. Owen's pirate flag is still flying next to the collection of pride flags that represent our family. Trans for me, bi for Meg, aro for Saint, gay for Owen, and ace for Carl and Nick. Baby handprints flutter next to the ornate key ornament Carl helped pick for Saint to give me when he asked us to move in for good. The gnome and angel from our first Christmas as a couple, and so many others.

"Pop, Saint's being mean to me." Meg turns her pout on me and I try to look sympathetic.

"I'm pretty sure you made the cut, kiddo." I smooth a hand over her short hair. The new look suits her. Makes her look so grown up that I can't help a pang at the fact this might be her last Christmas living at home with us. She's planning to go to university in Toronto, pre-law. Ready to take on the world and I couldn't be more proud of her. But the fact that things are going to change is inevitable. I'm going to miss these precious moments of being gathered together as a family like this.

Saint passes presents out to each of us. For the next little while, I just smile at the thought that went into each of the gifts. I could bask in the smiles on my kids' faces all day. I couldn't be more proud of my kiddos as they clear away the wrapping paper.

"Want us to help with the waffle bar?" Meg offers.

"I'll take care of the hash browns and cinnamon rolls," Owen chips in, fingers flying as he texts on his new phone. "Grating the potatoes and popping the cardboard tube is oddly satisfying."

"Mhm, hold that thought. There might be one last present." I appreciate the kids both offering to help with our traditional Christmas breakfast with Carl and Nick. Even if I'm pretty sure it will be forgotten in the excitement about Meg's last gift. It's one of those moments where it really sinks in that I'm so incredibly proud of the not-so-little humans I've raised. I'm hoarding these memories for when they're out living their lives in the coming years.

"Hm, looks like Santa didn't have much room in his sled for you, Meg, here." Saint tosses one last palm-sized box to her with a wink.

Meg looks between us, puzzled. "What's this?"

"Open it," I prompt her.

Meg does. Then she stares at the key fob, not quite comprehending. I suppose it looks similar to the spare key to the truck she's had since she got her license.

"You guys got me a Pikachu keychain?" Meg gives us a puzzled look. That was Saint's special touch to the present.

"Yep, just a keychain. What do you suppose that other thing dangling off it goes to?" Saint teases, eyes alight with humor.

"Get out!" Meg doesn't seem to quite believe the realization shining in her smile.

"Ah, sorry. No can do, darling. My therapist says I'm supposed to stick around and talk through conflicts," Saint teases. Meg is too excited to even roll her eyes at his corny humor. To be fair, he's worked hard at not pulling away from us when his insecurities get the best of him.

"No! You didn't?" Meg dances in place, not quite daring to fully embrace her glee. There's no way this would have been possible a few years ago. Saint offered to pay for the gift when I mentioned wanting Meg to be able to get home from university whenever she wants. For all his reservations about being a step-dad, he dotes on our kids like a giant sap. But Marcus knows his way around a vehicle, so he helped me find a reasonably priced, reliable used car.

"We did." I nod.

Saint winks. "Merry Christmas, kiddo."

Meg flings herself at us, hugging each of us in turn.

"Where is it? Can I see?" Meg asks.

"Pop's had it in the garage at Uncle Carl's all weekend," Owen says with a smirk, not looking up from texting his friends. Kid doesn't miss a thing. We're going to have to be sneakier when it's his turn. I don't want to think about my baby leaving the nest yet though, so I ignore that thought.

"Can I go take it for a test drive?" Meg pleads.

"Sure," I agree.

"I'll text Carl to open the garage." Saint tugs our girl into another hug, then he pulls out his phone.

"Ask when he and Nick are coming over for brunch," I remind Saint. That's become a tradition for us. That and a Christmas Eve movie marathon. Carl and Nick are as much family as Saint and my kids. So even if things are going to change, I'll be okay. Meg will never stop being my kid and owning a huge piece of my heart, no matter what bigger and better things she moves on to.

"Come on, loser! We're going cruising. If you play your cards right, I might even take you to see your boyfriend." Meg grabs her brother's arm.

"Shut up. For real?" Owen flushes at the attention on his relationship. He and Mikey have only been dating for a few months, but I've suspected he had a crush since before he came out to me, so that wasn't a surprise.

We all bundle up in jackets, boots, and toques to check out her car. Saint and I stand back, just drinking in Meg's exuberant appreciation of her gift, and the bond between my kids as they chatter excited plans to each other.

I field a few questions as Meg sits in the driver's seat with the window down, running her fingers over every surface like she's not sure it's real. Owen sits next to her and buckles in.

"We'll be back for brunch. Thanks, Pop and Saint!" Meg says as she rolls up the windows and backs carefully onto the road. Saint and I stand on the walkway in front of the duplex together.

"You did good with them." Saint wraps his arm around my waist and kisses my hair as we watch the kids drive off down the street.

"We're doing great," I agree, because I don't know how I'd have gotten through the past few years without his support and steady presence. I'd have made it work, but I don't know that we'd be thriving the way we are now.

"Helps that they're pretty much the best kids ever."

"We make a damn good team." I wink up at him, teasing.

"We do. Merry Christmas, Angel." Saint brushes the hair from my face. He kisses me there on the front steps. Like we're in one of Carl's sappy movies if not for the hand cupping my ass with promises for later, and I couldn't love this man more. There's no one else I want to spend all my Christmases loving.

THANKS FOR READING! IF you enjoyed Saint and Angel's love story, I would appreciate you taking the time to leave a review or rating to help other readers find .

Looking for Carl and Nick's story? Be sure to check out .

Want more single parent romance? Check out or .

For all the latest news about my sales and new releases, be sure to subscribe to my newsletter:

Other Works by Alex Silver

Merry Exmas

CONTEMPORARY CHRISTMAS ROMANCE

Table Topped

Contemporary Romance
Roll for Initiative (M/M) #1 Gui & Paz
Charisma Check (M/M) #2 Theo & Jude
Saving Throw (M/X) #3 Errol & Rene
Plus One Bonus (M/X) #4 Max & Si
Dump Stat (F/F) #5 Laura & Alice
Party of Three (M/M/X) #6 Pia, Emil, & Gregor
Balanced Party (M/M/X) #7 Pia, Emil, & Gregor

Summer of Adventures

Kinky Contemporary Romance
Dungeon Master (M/M)
Knotty Boy (M/M)
Service Call (M/M)
Picture Perfect (M/M)
Puppy Love (F/X)
Stud Muffin (M/M/M)

Hauntastic Haunts

M/M Paranormal Romance
Dan's Hauntastic Haunts Investigates:
Goodman Dairy *Book 1*
Hawk Lake *Book 2*
Ivarsson School *Book 3*
Joliet Asylum *Book 4*
Kapler Hotel *Book 5*

Free download links to the shorts are available in my FB group:

Drew's Haunted Hangout (*A Hauntastic Haunts Short Story 1)*

Rafael's Haunted Halloween (*A Hauntastic Haunts Short Story 2)*

Lee's Haunted Holiday (*A Hauntastic Haunts Short Story 3*)

Shift Work

Omegaverse MPreg Romance

Papa Bear (M/X)

Squirrel Trouble (M/M) (expanded edition)

Trash Panda (M/M)

Psions of SPIRE

Urban Fantasy

Shelter (M/M) Novella 0.5

Bright Spark (MMMM)Book 1

Bold Move (MMMM) Novella 1.5

Keen Sense (M/M) Book 2

Weak Link (M/M) Novella 2.5

Quick Fire (M/X) Book 3

Clear Sight (M/M) Book 4

New Look (M/M) Novella 4.5

A SPIREverse daddy kink standalone

New Ground (M/M/X)

Shared Universe Series

Super U - Superhero Romance
  Super U: Rising Storm (M/X)
  Final Days - Zombie Romance
  The Willows (M/M GNC)

Anthologies

Listen: The Sound of Fear
  Haunt (M/M trans gothic horror)
  Fix the World
  Upgrade (gay trans cyberpunk)

About the Author

ALEX SILVER (HE/THEM) GREW up mostly in Northern Maine and is now living in Canada with one spouse, two kids, and a lovebird. Alex is a trans guy who started writing fiction as a child and never stopped. Although there were detours through assisting on a farm and being a pharmacist along the way.

Visit me online at:

http://alexsilverauthor.wordpress.com/

Browse my entire book catalog at:

https://www.amazon.com/Alex-Silver/e/B07NPBW615

Join my Facebook group at:

https://www.facebook.com/groups/alexsalcove

Follow me on BookBub at:

https://www.bookbub.com/profile/alex-silver

Follow me on Twitter:

https://twitter.com/asilverauthor

Sign up for my for a free short story at:

And as always, consider leaving a review on Amazon or Goodreads if you enjoyed this book, reviews are of vital importance to independent authors, thanks!